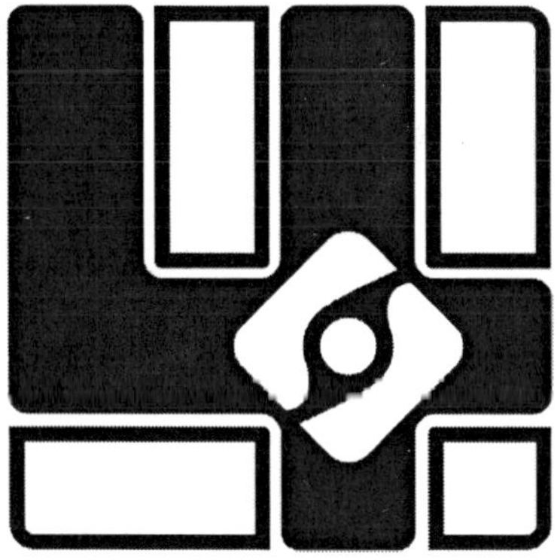

Warriors of the Balance

Samsun Lobe

Published by New Generation Publishing in 2016

First Edition

www.newgeneration-publishing.com

New Generation Publishing

For Barry, Trish, Jane and Mike

"We only have to look at ourselves to see how intelligent life might develop into something we wouldn't want to meet."

Stephen Hawking

The Old Enemy

The cockpit shook violently as the small craft materialised inside the cradle of the enormous jump gate. The small fighter was microscopic in comparison to the skeletal arms that hung down around it. They resembled steel ribs arching out from a colossal and complex mechanical spine.

The jump gates provided almost instant travel across the Shakari galaxy. Initially few in number, they were crude and restrictive in construction but their invention had allowed the Prime worlds to explore and colonise space. Now more than seven thousand years since their inception, a vast network linked the many star systems that formed the Federation of United Republics - FOUR.

A blue glow popped into life around the outlet cones of the small craft's fusion engines. The blackness seemed to fold in around them as the attached density drives fired and the tiny fighter started to accelerate forwards. The fusion engine provided the propulsion and the density drives had the job of altering the molecular volume of the craft, the faster it went the lighter it became.

There was no mistaking the purpose of the compact spacecraft. To kill. The whole design was aggressive in look and function. Gaping barrels of lethal Volt cannons were slung under the nose and two more arranged side by side, occupied a blister turret under the rear fuselage. The ship had arched wings that jutted out from behind the cockpit. In the shadows beneath them sat an arsenal of projectiles. The whole thing resembled a mechanical hornet. It was called the Apocris.

It was the personal transport of Ecclesiarch Srisk Montellar. He was a servant of the veiled Noxvata. He was a clandestine warrior of the balance. A myth. A bringer of death.

Srisk twisted the wrench in his hand to tighten the hex bolt on the forefinger of his left gauntlet. The power armour he wore was new, as his old suit had suffered catastrophic failure on his previous mission. He missed it. Despite its antiquated technology and lack of features, it just felt better. The new armour seemed to have constant glitches and the need for permanent adjustment. Maybe he just preferred old things, or maybe it was all in his mind. Maybe his mind was as mutilated as his body.

As he moved his arms he felt the tightness of fresh scar tissue across his chest and inside his ribcage. He had nearly died in his last encounter. Perhaps that would have been a blessing. He had served his masters, the Noxvata, for centuries. He had followed their every word, preaching their laws and delivering their justice. He knew they no longer trusted him, that he was no longer their champion of choice. It didn't matter. He had never served from loyalty or for a higher purpose. He served because he carried the guilt of a lost civilisation. He served to atone for his perceived sins.

He looked out from beneath his heavy black hood at the small scarlet reptilian creature that sat in the pilot's position. Its long tail poked out through the back of the chair. Srisk ran his gauntleted fingers along the frayed edge of his cloak. It was the one thing that he had salvaged from his old suit. It had no place alongside the modern power armour; it was a relic from a forgotten world. It gave him comfort as well as hiding his countenance from view. Only the pallid orange glow of his augmented eyes were visible in the dark recess of his face.

"How long?"

Srisk's voice was a mechanised monotone, devoid of emotion. The small creature looked over its shoulder. The green and blue hues of the cockpit lighting danced across its bulbous eyes.

"Not long Master. We are entering the Katayama System now. Approximately twenty-six hours, forty-two minutes and thirty-one seconds until we reach orbit over Kalleeka.

"That's approximate?"

"There is always a chance of an unforeseen event Master. Things change."

Srisk smiled an unseen smile. 'How true' he thought. He had saved the small reptilian creature some years back. The Noxvata had wanted it balanced. He had disobeyed them. The red creature was no threat to anyone. He had an uncanny knack with technology and could pilot the Apocris adeptly. Better even than the Ecclesiarch himself. The creature's name was Liktus.

"Master?" The question trailed off. Srisk knew this was the start of an inquiry.

"What is it Liktus?"

"Apart from our destination you've not told me anything about this mission. Should I be concerned?"

"No more than usual" replied Srisk.

"You do know that your need for theatrical mystery is not helpful?"

"Neither is this inquisition."

The servos in Srisk's armour whirred as he pulled himself up in his chair. He had worked alone since he had left his home world in the distant past. He had refused the Noxvata's continued calls for him to lead a team. He didn't want that burden. If things went awry, then he only had himself to blame. He didn't want the responsibility for others. His heart had no more room for guilt.

Liktus held his stare. His eyelids closed and slowly opened, his gaze piercing the Ecclesiarch's hooded cowl. The creature's lip curled in an awkward smile.

"Wake me when we arrive. I will make a jump from the thermosphere" declared Srisk.

"This is a category four planet Master. I can land safely on the surface. They do not possess the technology to detect our presence."

"As always my scarlet friend you are right, but things change."

*

The short transition from the cockpit into the rear fuselage was awkward. Srisk was almost seven feet tall. Encased from head to toe in power armour added another foot. The narrow neck of the ship caused him to knock and bang his elbows and shoulders as he made his way through. Srisk thought it was about time he dulled the newness of his suit. He almost fell into the cargo hold and breathed out as he stood upright. The rear of the ship was designed to carry six fully armoured soldiers. It was empty apart from Srisk's equipment. He grabbed the large whisper rifle and mag-locked it to his back along with his molecular sword.

His suit would allow him to survive in the airless environment but to slow the long descent to the planet's surface he would need additional help. The motors in his arms and legs whined as he hoisted a burner pack above his head and clamped it down onto his shoulders. His mind automatically acknowledged the additional equipment and a small icon blipped on his ocular head-up-display. Srisk was cybernetically linked with all of his gear. A simple thought was all it took to operate it. His Recit crackled into life.

"Can you hear me Master?"

"All clear" replied Srisk.

"What are your instructions Master?"

"How long is a day on this world?"

"Thirty hours Master."

"In that case, remain in orbit and then come and get me in four days. That should be plenty."

There was a moment's silence.

"What if that's not enough time Master?"

"If that is the case, then you are relieved from my employ and free to do as you so choose."

Liktus did not reply.

"Open the bay door" instructed Srisk.

Pistons hissed as the door popped its seal and the air was sucked from the hold in a nanosecond. Srisk's magnetic boots clanked against the chequer plate as the orange halo of Kalleeka filled the view. Without another word Srisk dived into the alien world.

Srisk's destination was pre-programmed into his nav-system and the shoulder mounted jet-pack flared to steer his descent.

Exploring new worlds had once held excitement and trepidation for the long serving Ecclesiarch, but even the magnificent view of the orange and red planet failed to stir his emotions. Perhaps that was another thing he had lost forever.

As he slid through the stratosphere, he felt an increase in heat due to the thicker air. He made a mental adjustment to his shield and cooling systems. The shoulder jets fired slowing his speed. One of the vents spluttered and a warning node pulsed in Srisk's eye indicating its failure. The Ecclesiarch employed a technique he had learned over his many years in the field and thumped the jet with his fist. It sparked, coughed and then re-ignited.

The rest of his descent went unhindered. He surveyed the landscape of the category four world. All known worlds in the Shakari galaxy had been classified. Category or level four meant that there was an intelligent life form in existence but as yet they had not evolved any significant technology.

Massive mountain ranges stretched around the orange globe. They were the only visible geography. The rest of the world seemed devoid of all features. Vast deserts sprawled across the majority of the surface. Only the occasional black stain pockmarked the smooth landscape. Srisk started to wonder if this was another mission of subterfuge by the Noxvata. Were they sending him here to his death? Probably, he surmised.

The jet-pack roared and swallowed the last of its fuel. The immense sudden burn slowed the metal clad warrior and his leg hydraulics extended to absorb the impact. Srisk thudded into the sandy desert. Dust swirled skyward and as the Ecclesiarch straightened he released the mag-lock on his pack and it smashed into the ground. The landscape was flat and featureless in every direction. The surface was baked and cracked and dust devils danced with each other. Srisk held his forearm in front of him and a holographic map fizzed into view. He was in the right location, at least the location he had been given. There was nothing here. There was nothing for miles. He had seen a mountain range far to the North as he had descended. That seemed like a logical destination.

Srisk's long cloak billowed behind him as the giant warrior strode across the desert. His eyes constantly scanning the horizon for any signs of life. The heat haze was hampering his optics. He had walked in a straight line for three hours and had seen nothing but dried mud and sand. Eventually far in the distance the mountain peaks came into view. They looked as if they floated in the sky as the reflected heat created a band of illusion. Srisk cycled the filters on his ocular implants. He had thought he had noticed movement. Thermal was unusable as was infra-red and ultra-violet. He toggled the view to a de-saturated spectrum. It was the clearest view yet. He had been correct. There was movement ahead. He reached to his back and grabbed the pistol grip of the huge whisper rifle. The gun was almost as tall as the Ecclesiarch. It was a type of assault rail gun. It fired magnetic projectiles and super-sonic speed. It also came equipped with an under slung explosive launcher and a powerful set of scopes. Srisk knelt down with one knee and placed his elbow on the other holding the rifle steady. He linked to the scope with his mind and zoomed in on the image. Srisk cursed. At least the Noxvata had been correct about one thing.

Through the scope he could see what he deduced was a female native of Kalleeka running for her life. She was small, bipedal and her skin was a similar red to Liktus. She had piercing golden eyes and her dust covered face was streaked with tears. Her long black matted hair trailed behind her as she ran. It was the creature that pursued her that had got Srisk's attention. It was Moretti and it was a Marauder.

The early history of the Galaxy recorded several skirmishes between the Prime worlds as they reached out into space, but a lasting peace had followed coupled with the integrated expansion of those races. It wasn't until the arrival of the Moretti that everything changed. They flooded into the Extomis Arm of the galaxy destroying everything they encountered. Srisk's home planet of Ventor was one of the first Prime worlds to succumb. The Moretti were an unstoppable force. They seemed to have no other agenda other than expansion and destruction. World after world fell under their onslaught. The remaining Prime worlds were forced to collaborate and the fledgling alliance of the Federation was born. The combined might was enough to stem the rampaging tide of the Moretti. The ebb and flow of conflict consumed everything in the West of the galaxy, until one day the Moretti suddenly and inexplicably stopped their advance. Whether that was due to the actions of the Federation was unknown. Some concluded that the Moretti had spread themselves too thinly and were fighting in other galaxies. Whatever the reason the thousand years of bloodshed subsided. The Moretti remained in the worlds they had conquered but their lust for conquest had been extinguished. An exclusion zone was enforced by the Federation to act as a buffer which became known as Dark Space. Massive gun platforms and moon-sized space stations were built to protect the Federation allies. It was known as the Defensive Necklace. It remains unused.

Srisk had fought the Moretti on his home world before it had been overrun. He had enlisted in the Federation army of Theocentricus and battled the fearsome foe for another hundred years before his induction into the employ of the Noxvata. He knew firsthand what lethal killers they were. The Noxvata had promised him revenge on the enemy that had slaughtered his people. They had delivered on that promise. Srisk had killed countless Moretti. When the war ended the Noxvata slid into the shadows and now pulled the strings in the galactic politics of the Primes. Srisk knew there was much more to the nebulous organisation than would ever be revealed.

That the Moretti had once again decided to show themselves was a serious concern. The fact they were here on an inconsequential world inside Federation space was confusing. It was the reason the Noxvata had sent him. To return to the Ninth Cloud with the leader of the Moretti force on Kalleeka. A Guardian.

In his years fighting the Moretti, Srisk had studied his foe in depth. They were upright bipedal creatures, most in excess of six feet tall. They had bony extrusions covering their bodies like they wore their skeletons on the outside. Their jet black eyes contrasted the pale white outer carapace and gave them the appearance of the living dead. They were powerful, determined and skilful fighters but their main strength came in overwhelming numbers. Every time Srisk had met them in battle he had been awed as wave upon wave of the rampaging foe poured into the fray. Thousands upon thousands. No matter how many they killed, more came.

Not much was known about their social make up. All that was known was that there were different kinds of Moretti:

The Paragons: Mythical leaders of the Moretti. None had ever been seen, they were known in rumours only. Guardians: The strongest and most intelligent of the Moretti. They formed the backbone of command. Thankfully there were very few of this type of warrior. The Thornbred: those that made up the majority of the ground troops and wore spiky armour. The Sentinels: taller than the other Moretti were believed to be able to organise the forces telepathically, linking the horde as one entity. The Resonators: formed the support duties of the main force. They operated the bio-mechanical weapons, artillery and controlled the terrifying beasts that often accompanied the larger armies. The Marauders: they were infantry. Unlike their compatriots, the Thornbred, they chose to face their enemies without armour. They daubed themselves with unreadable obscenities, and these bare-chested, bone clad warriors were often the first to the fight. It was one of these soldiers that was closing on the native female ahead.

Srisk's finger hovered over the trigger. His reticule lined up on the forehead of the sprinting Marauder. This was not his fight. It would just complicate his mission. If the indigenous population had endured any time at all under the yoke of the Moretti then a swift death for this woman would be a blessing. He looked back through the sight. The Marauder had caught the female. She was scrambling on her hands and knees in the dust. The painted warrior removed a hooked sword from his back and raised it over his head. Srisk looked away.

A second later he pulled the trigger. A faint thwip resounded from the rifle as the solid round left the barrel. An instant later the back of the Moretti's head erupted in a fountain of blood, brain and bone.

The scarlet skinned female sat in a stunned trance. Staring motionless as the dead body of the Marauder slowly fell to its knees and then face first into the desert floor. She then turned quickly trying to ascertain from which direction the saving shot had originated. Srisk had made the shot at well over a mile and half. She could not see him, even if she had known in what direction she should have looked.

The Ecclesiarch returned the whisper rifle to his back and started to lope across the desert towards his kill. With his enhanced suit and his long stride he closed the distance in less than three minutes. The female had seen him coming and had fumbled for the dead creature's side arm. She struggled to hold the heavy weapon out in front of her.

"I mean you no harm" announced Srisk.

The female frowned from her lack of comprehension.

"Get away from me" she warned. Her language was a derivative of the Seeda System. Srisk's audible implants quickly translated her speech, not that he needed speech to communicate. Srisk was a powerful telepath. He reached out to the nativc.

< I mean you no harm > he repeated.

"How are you doing that?" said the frightened woman.

< You are hearing my thoughts. It is nothing to fear. It will be a few more moments before my implants adjust to your language >

The woman scrambled backwards still levelling the pistol at the Ecclesiarch.

"That's better" declared Srisk. The female's golden eyes widened.

"I can understand you" she stammered.

"As I explained. It takes a few moments for my vocal chords to attune." Srisk noticed the bite and claw marks covering her legs and arms. The Moretti had been using her for sport. "You can lower that weapon. It won't do you any good." He leant forward and reached out to take the gun. The female pulled the trigger. The pistol clicked as if it were empty. Srisk gently pried her fingers away and took the gun. He swivelled and threw it out into the desert. "Their weapons are organically linked. Only a Moretti can fire a Moretti weapon."

"You are not one of them then?" asked the woman.

"No my dear. I dare say I am something much worse. However I am not here to harm you. I am here to find the creature that leads the others of this kind." Srisk indicated towards the dead body. "My name is Srisk."

The female scrambled to her feet and dusted down her ragged clothes.

"I am Lelani. The one you seek has taken the Sacred Spires." She pointed to the mountains in the distance.

"Thank you" said Srisk. "Tell me Lelani how did you escape?"

The red skinned female looked sadly towards the ground.

"They arrived less than twenty moons ago. They killed without mercy. Those that did not escape to the tundra were held captive in the Spires. They killed my family. They killed everyone" Tears once again ran down her dirt encrusted cheeks.

"They are without conscience" said Srisk.

"They used the rest of us as sport. They made us run into the desert. They used us as target practice. The plain that lies before the Spires is a field of carnage. I ran as the moon rose and ran through the night. I thought I had escaped." Once more tears welled in her eyes. "Why? Why have they done this?"

"That is what I am here to discover" assured Srisk. "And my dear Lelani, you have escaped." A brief smile illuminated her dusty features. The female reached out and took hold of Srisk's metal gauntlet.

"How will you kill them all? You are just one."

Srisk wasn't prepared to tell her he was only here for a certain individual. It was not his remit to engage the entire Moretti force on this planet. When he left this place, she would die, as would eventually the rest of her kind. Even if the Federation knew of the Moretti's presence here, they would be cautious in their approach. Another war was something they would avoid at all costs. Even if that meant sacrificing an entire world.

"It only takes one person to turn out the lights" replied Srisk.

"What does that mean?" asked Lelani.

"It is an old saying from my past. It means that it only takes one person to plunge a world into darkness."

"Then you promise you will kill them?" begged Lelani.

"I will do what I can" answered Srisk.

"Then come with me. I can show the way to the mountains."

*

The strange couple walked for almost an hour in a Westerly direction. Srisk had suggested that they were moving away from the mountains, but was happy to be reassured by his native guide. Kalleeka's star was high in the sky and Srisk's suit was struggling to keep him cool. The sooner they could get to the shade of the mountains the better. His small companion seemed completely unfazed by the intense heat. She reached into her tunic and took out a small mirror. She placed the instrument on the ground and lay down to look into it. She scrambled to her feet and paced around the area staring at the ground like she had lost something. Lelani spotted what she was after and ran ahead. She moved a thin covering of sand with her feet to reveal a flat stone. She did the same thing again slowly revealing an obscure pattern set into the slab.

"I'll need your help" she said looking back to the confused Ecclesiarch.

He strode to her location and then noticed the strange stone set into the floor. Srisk cycled his sensors surveying the horizon. There was nothing to detect. He bent down and lifted the slab clear. Dust swirled into the humid air forming a mini vortex before suddenly collapsing into the hole that he had uncovered.

Srisk peered into the shaft. It had been hewn from the solid bedrock. Semi-circular recesses had been carved into the walls and Lelani was already climbing down using them. She beckoned him to follow.

The Ecclesiarch's power armour hissed as he leapt into the pit. More compressed air vented as his suit took the shock of landing. Dust and debris filled the immediate area as the huge warrior's armour started to illuminate in the gloom. He needed no help to see in the dark, but the system reacted automatically to the low light level. They moved into the tunnel away from the rectangular beam of light from above.

"Can you switch those off?" asked Lelani.

"Of course" replied Srisk instantly plunging them into a temporary darkness. Several moments later the Ecclesiarch became aware of a subtle illumination. He reached out a finger and touched the bioluminescence that coated the walls and ceiling. His suits sensors sampled the substance.

"Bacteria" said Srisk.

"I don't know what that is" said Lelani. "We call it Soulfire"

"Of course" acknowledged Srisk.

Ahead of them the tunnels opened out. There was a large cavern with multiple offshoots, some showed evidence of tooling marks whilst others were scoured smooth. He walked forward and reached up to touch the circular roof.

"Some of these were made by water" he observed.

"Yes" said Lelani. "Our Songwords say that once our home was covered in water. That it flowed through the ground making these passageways."

"Do you still have water?" asked Srisk.

Lelani looked suspiciously at the metal clad warrior. Srisk could sense her reticence.

"I understand" explained Srisk. "On a desert world, water would be a most valuable commodity; you do not need to answer."

"They are sacred sites" confessed Lelani.

"Of course" agreed Srisk. "Do you have anything else of value?"

Again Lelani was suspicious of the question.

"For example do you mine precious metals, stones or liquids. I am trying to discern possible reasons as to why the Moretti would risk a war by coming to this place.

"Maybe they don't care" suggested Lelani.

"More than likely" admitted Srisk.

The Ecclesiarch turned to his side and suddenly thousands of minute drones buzzed upwards in a swarm. Lelani jumped backwards. The cloud of drones quickly flew ahead, dissolving into smaller groups as they reached each tunnel intersection.

"What were they?" asked a stunned Lelani.

"I am assuming this labyrinth of tunnels will lead to the mountain range. They were tiny sensors. They will map this cave system and send the data to my navigation system."

"I will show you the way" insisted Lelani.

"I know you will, but I never do anything without a contingency plan."

Judging by the blank expression on her face, it was clear to see she had no idea what he was talking about. The two companions made their way deeper into the cavern. Srisk stopped at regular intervals to allow the returning drones access to his suit.

Srisk ducked through a low opening and stepped into a large cavern. The ground fell away sharply and the trickle of water could be heard from below. The incandescent light illuminated a crude stone bridge that crossed the chasm. Lelani was already half way across. She stopped and turned to the alien warrior.

"Are you from the same place as the Bone Devils?"

"Where do you believe they are from?"

"From across the sea" said Lelani.

Srisk smiled at the reference and at the innocence of a civilisation that had yet to think beyond the limits of the planet that gave them life.

"By sea, I assume you mean the dustbowl we were walking across?"

"Yes obviously" said Lelani.

"I am not from across the sea, nor am I from the same place as the Bone Devils."

"Then where are you from?"

"That is not an easy question to answer."

The Ecclesiarch knelt onto the stone bridge. He drew two circles with his finger.

"This is your star. This..." he pointed to the second circle. "Is your planet. When you look to the night sky, what do you see?" he asked.

"Lights. Thousands of lights."

"They are stars. Like the one that heats your world. Most of them have a planet like yours. I am from one of them. Far away from here. The Bone Devils are also from across the stars."

Lelani looked up into his dark hood. A wide grin spread across her face.

"Sure" she said still smiling. "Why do you hide your face?" she said suddenly.

Srisk stood.

"Some things need to remain hidden."

Suddenly the Ecclesiarch spun as his motion sensors flashed on his ocular head-up display. He dropped to his knee as the Thornbred warrior rushed from the darkness. The lone Moretti's serrated blade passed over his shoulder pad tearing a strip from his cloak. An instant later a solid round thumped into his chest armour knocking Srisk onto his back. Several more whistled over his prone form before the Ecclesiarch reached out and grabbed the Thornbred soldier who was recovering from over-stretching. Srisk reached to his back and the hilt of his mag-locked molecular sword thumped into his gauntlet. It hummed as it came to life.

It had two modes of operation: One which produced a crackling electrical field. The second, its main function, caused the molecules of the metal to vibrate at impossibly high frequencies. The moving edge would then cut through anything as it separated the molecules of anything it came into contact with. It was an old, crude weapon, but very effective.

Srisk rammed the wide, almost cleaver-like blade up into the Moretti's ribcage. The edge shimmered as if it skipped between realities. It slid with ease through the soldier's Graphene armour cleaving his life-core in two. Srisk pulled the dead body towards him as a salvo of rounds thundered from the darkness. The Thornbred's armour spalled and splintered as multiple slugs thumped into it. Srisk's arm servos wheezed as he flung it forward throwing his sword at his hidden attackers. He knew the Moretti would avoid its path, but he needed time. Just a nanosecond. His optics cycled to infrared and the heat signatures of four soldiers popped into view.

The Ecclesiarch slid his whisper rifle into his hand and pulled the trigger. At such close range he didn't need to aim. Several dozen magnetic rounds punched holes through the surprised Moretti. They were used to their armour repelling the majority of ammunition.

Srisk stumbled forward as two more slugs hammered into his back plate. Cursing, he pivoted and threw the dead warrior he had been using as a shield out towards the two approaching Moretti. Swinging his rifle down onto his other hand, he pumped the lower mechanism and a high explosive round shot out. It exploded as it hit the lifeless body of the Thornbred warrior disintegrating his carcass and sending fragments of his armour into the two other soldiers. The force of the blast caused the thin stone bridge to crumble and the rearguard Moretti disappeared in a plume of dust, shattered bone and blood.

Srisk span. Rolling to his right he avoided a poorly aimed shot from one of the remaining injured soldiers. The aging Ecclesiarch closed the distance in a second and kicked out at the warrior sending him flying back into the cavern wall. Srisk cycled his optics once again. Two of the Moretti Thornbred were already dead. One was trying to crawl away and the last was trying to stand after his impact with the rock wall. The Ecclesiarch stalked towards him and levelled the barrel of his gun against the warrior's spiked helm. A single round smashed through the soldier's brain and buried itself deep in the bedrock behind.

Srisk reached down and retrieved his still humming sword. He strode towards the last warrior. The Moretti was struggling to move his weight with one arm. The Ecclesiarch's rounds had shattered his left arm and pelvis. Srisk flipped him over with his foot. With a finessed precision he swiped the molecular blade across the side of the soldier's helm. The painted visor fell away revealing the jet black eyes, and the white, bone clad face of the Thornbred.

"Anach vey molessen" The words spat from the dying soldier's mouth like acid.

Srisk replayed the message on his Recit. It was a form of Moretti speech he had not encountered before. He knew they spoke in various dialects and over time had added many to his language database. The audio diagnostics quickly decoded the unique speech patterns. It translated as: "War is coming."

The Ecclesiarch looked into the dark eyes of the Moretti. He would tell him nothing more. They were hardened soldiers; no amount of torture would loosen its vile tongue. Not even Srisk's telepathic skill could unlock the warped mind of the Moretti.

The Ecclesiarch knelt down so that his hooded face was all that the stubborn Thornbred could see.

"I will be ready"

Srisk slid the wide blade into the soldier's core and twisted the handle. He watched as pain was replaced by euphoria and then finally life fled from the soldier's glassy eyes.

The whole encounter had taken less than twenty seconds. It was as if it had happened in slow motion. He scanned the chasm below to ensure the two Moretti that had fallen were dead. He detected two lifeless bodies. The third warrior was scattered throughout the cave. The Ecclesiarch knew that Lelani was gone. He heard a faint scream. The sound came from the labyrinth of tunnels that lay ahead. She was still alive. At least for the moment.

FOUR - Warriors of the Balance -Samsun Lobe

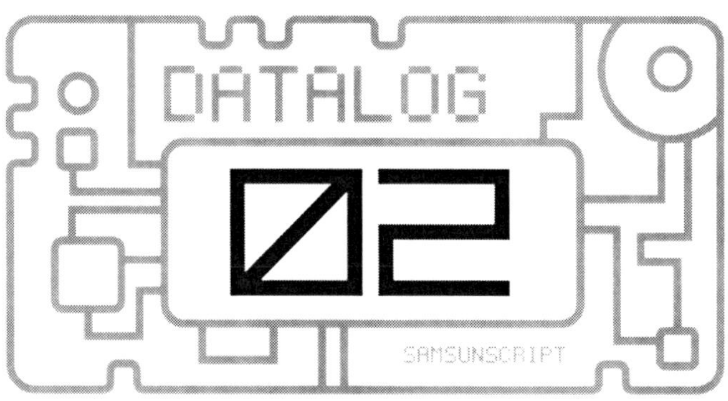

The Ninth Cloud

Intelligence was the key to any mission. Whether it involved stealth or a frontal assault, whether it was a handful of combatants or a war of nations. Srisk understood this more than most. He had survived countless battles. He assured himself it was due totally to his preparedness. Others might have said he had divine favour.

The vast tunnel complex beneath the baked surface crust provided too many ambush locations for the Ecclesiarch's liking. He had waited until nightfall before returning to the desert and making his way to the rocky spires under the cover of darkness.

*

The light from the great star Katayama intensified below the horizon signalling the start of a new day. A dull red glow started to cast its long shadows across the arid environment.

Srisk had not slept, but his reconnaissance was now complete. The mountain range which he had seen as he descended from the upper atmosphere was actually a vast complex of hand carved buildings. The native population had used the natural rock formations and burrowed their living structures into them. Windows, doors and pillared openings peppered the rock face. Bridges linked some of the taller rock stacks and a defensive wall linked the lower reaches of the mountain. Srisk had surmised that due to its construction and location it had once been a harbour wall, keeping a long forgotten sea from ravaging the inner reaches of the city. The structure was basic, almost primitive. In the radiance of the morning light, it reminded the Ecclesiarch of a magnificent Termitious mound, albeit without movement. The Moretti had seen to that.

In their unequalled efficiency they had invaded and eradicated the native population. The reason for which still eluded the Ecclesiarch. Why would the Moretti enter Federation space? They knew it would provoke war if they were discovered. Maybe the fragile peace was about to shatter. The problem with the situation was the planet itself. It provided no strategic advantage. They were a long way inside the Defensive Necklace plus it was too close to the Prime worlds of Shankara and Anu. Any Moretti force intending to use this as a bridgehead or forward base would be quickly engulfed by the overwhelming power of FOUR.

His mission from the Noxvata had been simple. Travel to Kalleeka. Find the Moretti Guardian and bring him back to the Ninth Gate for questioning. The Lords of the Balance had ways of extracting information that were known only to the inner conclave. They had assured him that the Moretti force would be minimal. In that they were correct. As far as the Ecclesiarch could ascertain this was a rapid assault squad consisting of twenty two remaining soldiers, plus the eight he had already dispatched. The problem was the Guardian. Srisk knew the Moretti better than most. The Guardian were elites among their kind. They would command legions of a hundred thousand soldiers. It was beneath such a creature to lead a small strike group, even with the safety of such a non developed world. There was much more to this situation than the Ecclesiarch could define. The political impact of his mission would have to wait as Srisk's attention was drawn to the defensive wall below. From his lofty vantage point he zoomed in on the several soldiers that had appeared. They were all Thornbred. Three of them. They were holding long pulse rifles and looking out over the wall towards the desert.

The area in front of the once great harbour wall was covered in small bumps. Thousands of them. Srisk zoomed in further, and then looked away in disgust. They were bodies. Most had been covered by the swirling desert sands, but several fresh kills showed the catastrophic wounds of plasma rifles. Some were missing limbs others had dark red holes the size of a fist punched through their naked flesh. It was far worse than Lelani had described. As Srisk turned back he heard the fizz of gunfire. He watched as a terrified native darted across the body strewn wasteland. The molten round exploded next to him sending sharp shards into the air. The heat of the plasma turned the sand to glass and it made lethal shrapnel as it shattered. Several pieces sliced into the legs of the young man. He stumbled briefly before another round hit him in the shoulder and sent him spinning him from his feet. He was dead before his limp body slammed into the ground.

Two of the soldiers on the wall held their rifles high in the air and celebrated by clashing their guns against each other. The remaining Thornbred thumped his nearest colleague in the arm and pointed out towards the tundra where two more natives ran for their lives. They quickly scrabbled to take aim. The furthest Moretti soldier turned the dials on his rifle attempting to dial in his sights but then suddenly staggered to his right. Brown blood pumped from a gaping hole in the side of his head. The two remaining soldiers swivelled seeking out their attacker. A quiet thwip, thwip whispered on the breeze as two magnetic rounds smashed into the body of one of the stunned Thornbreds. The rounds made a small entry wound but exploded on exit. The second shot almost decapitated the soldier. The force of the impact threw him back over the wall. The last warrior ran for cover. Srisk took aim and gently squeezed the trigger. The round hit the fleeing soldier in the side of the knee, skittling him sideways. Sensors flashed on Srisk's HUD. He acknowledged the incoming ordinance but not before releasing a final round.

He didn't need to see the shot hit its target. He knew it would. He also knew that the morning show he had just witnessed had been designed for his benefit. It had been fabricated to draw him out of his hiding position so that the two soldiers positioned in opposite spires and armed with venom rockets had a clear shot. It was a good plan, but Srisk had allowed for that outcome. The wire rope complained as the heavy Ecclesiarch abseiled from the rocky crag. He braced for impact and he feathered the brake. As he thumped to the ground the rock stack above him exploded as the two rockets hit their target. Srisk vaulted through a hole he had made previously and ducked into safety as several tonnes of debris rained down. He smiled to himself and then sent the command: <Destruct>

One of the rocket wielding Moretti twisted as he heard the high pitch bleep behind him. He only had time to open his mouth in disbelief before the explosive charge evaporated his position. A simultaneous muffled whump echoed across the stone spires as the second rocket emplacement imploded and a dust cloud enveloped the top of the rock stack.

Srisk was already deep inside the city making his way towards the central chapel. It was the only section he had not scouted in the night. It had to be home to the Guardian. Nothing else in the underground complex was large enough. He still had some way to go through the narrow passages. His progress was hampered further as he was dragging three stolen pieces of Moretti equipment.

Finally he reached the intersection outside of the chapel entrance. The crudely carved doors were almost grandiose in comparison to the rest to the city's decor.

Inset into the stone floor was a circular pool. There were steps down into the greenish water. It was the perfect location thought Srisk. He hurriedly set up the equipment. He had taken the three units from the Moretti store in the night. He had searched the complex for a landing craft but found none. The invaders had unloaded everything they thought they may need and left it unguarded. Sloppy.

Each unit was mounted on a tripod and the Ecclesiarch flicked out the legs and placed each one around the pool. He thumped the magazine on one of them as it didn't look as if it was seated correctly. Srisk heard a comforting click. He switched on each machine and then broke radio silence and squelched his Recit. He knew the Moretti would be scanning for any communications. They would be here soon enough. Srisk stepped into the pool and slid beneath the surface. He held his breath and mentally started to shut down his suit. He wanted absolute quiet. More than that he needed it. He held a remote in his power gauntlet. His finger hovered over the flashing button.

He heard footsteps. Heavy. Thornbred. He waited as they drew closer. They would stop soon. As soon as they saw the machines they would stop. He waited. The footsteps skidded to a halt and voices shouted. Srisk pressed the button. The three machines barked into life. They were antipersonnel mines. Each held a vertical canister of two hundred palm sized discs. The unit spat these razor sharp projectiles out at phenomenal speed. Worse than that the small silver discs homed in on sound. Any sound, no matter how minute. Even the breath output from a Moretti helmet, or the creak of an armour joint. Srisk held his breath completely motionless as the units emptied their contents into the corridors. Only after he had heard the empty cyclic clicking did the Ecclesiarch emerge from the water.

Scanning the dust strewn tunnels he detected disjointed movement. He launched an explosive round in all three directions closing the way in and the way out. Holding his rifle against his shoulder he slowly pushed open the door to the chapel.

Large pillars lined the impressive space and held up the carved ceiling above. Towering almost half their height stood the Guardian. Light flooded down around him from a gaping hole in the roof. Srisk surmised it was how he had got in, as his bulk would not have made it through the tunnels. He was enormous. Almost three times Srisk's height. He had encountered a Guardian before, but only from a distance. Up close the creature was magnificent. He wore obsidian black armour with silver detail covering every edge and fold. A large silver Moretti skull was emblazoned across his chest. He wore no helm, instead the bone plates of his head had been engraved and inlaid with silver. In one hand he held a long war maul. The head of the giant hammer crackled with arcane power. In the other hand he held the tiny form of Lelani. He tilted his head slightly to one side as if sizing up his opponent. The Guardian smiled revealing a hideous set of pointed black teeth. Each one was as long as Srisk's fingers.

"Welcome emissary" His deep voice boomed across the chapel. Srisk understood the greeting as the Moretti commander had spoken in the tongue of the Noxvata - High Sangelon. He continued his greeting.

" I am Murac' Amor. Devastator of the Thousand Suns. Was there really any need for this show. I realise I said I would be alone, but these men were just my personal retinue."

Srisk composed himself. He met Lelani's gaze as she struggled in the giant's grip. The Guardian noticed the look and cast an inquiring glance towards the female and then back at Srisk.

"Do these people have meaning to you?" asked Murac' Amor

"I abhor the senseless loss of life" replied Srisk smoothly.

Booming laughter echoed through the chamber.

"My men were only amusing themselves whilst we waited for you. These people mean nothing." He held Lelani out towards the Ecclesiarch "Look. This is a worthless bag of bones. They are not even worthy of the Federation, much less the Lords of the Balance."

With a simple twitch of his wrist he snapped Lelani's neck. The Guardian threw her dead body into the gloom.

"Enough pleasantries emissary. Where is the key?"

Srisk scanned the darkness for signs of life. Nothing. Srisk remained calm.

"What is it that my masters have promised you? inquired Srisk.

"Do not play games with me errand boy"

"You would risk war with the Federation for the key?" probed Srisk having no clue what the key was. Whatever the Noxvata had agreed with the Moretti Guardian they had omitted in their briefing to the Ecclesiarch. He needed to know what his masters were up to. He would keep the rouse going for as long as he could.

"War? What are you talking about? The Moretti will not wage war until the mourning for our beloved Ensut' Kala is over. Your masters know this. It is why they have promised us the key. I can tell from your procrastination that you do not have it. You are playing a dangerous game."

"I believe we are both being played" confessed Srisk. He could hear footsteps and falling rubble behind him. He turned to see the remaining five members of the assault team enter the chapel. One of them was a Marauder. He was bare-chested and had symbols painted over the white bone plates that covered his dark skin. He also had two red streaks daubed vertically down over each eye. He snarled as he walked past the Ecclesiarch. He bowed low to the Guardian.

"Great Murac' Amor."

"Is that an apology?" said the Guardian moving forward encasing the kneeling Marauder in shadow.

"I do not have an excuse."

Without warning the giant hammer in Murac' Amor's hand sparked to life and in a mind spinning blur thumped into the floor obliterating the bowing Moretti. The Guardian withdrew the maul and the electrical field subsided. The blow had reduced the body to a lump of meat and a viscous liquid pooled in the depression the hammer had made. Murac' Amor turned his attention back to Srisk. The Ecclesiarch heard the click of the rifles pointed at his back. His plan had been well executed until this point. Now it was time for improvisation.

"If you do not have the key. Then why are you here? What is your errand?"

Srisk tabbed through his suits functions and status. It was at eighty percent. He had eighty seven mag rounds, and a single explosive round in his whisper rifle.

"My instructions were to bring you back to Sangelon" admitted Srisk.

The Guardian smiled.

"And exactly how were you going to do that?" grinned Murac' Amor.

"I was beginning to wonder that myself" said Srisk. "I am not sure you would fit in the hold of my ship. Perhaps I will have to take you back in pieces."

Now the Guardian laughed. The deep bass of his voice bounced around the cavernous chapel.

"I admire your optimism, although I am confused as to why an individual of your obvious courage chooses to hide behind a hood."

One of the soldiers behind him made to grab for the back of his cloak. Srisk rammed his elbow backwards shattering the face plate of the shocked Thornbred. He staggered and then angrily levelled his plasma rifle against Srisk's head.

"Enough!" bellowed Murac' Amor. The soldier reluctantly stood down. "It does not matter. We all have our secrets Ventorian."

The word stung Srisk like a poisoned dart. He had not been called that for a long time. He cursed his own failings. He had lowered his mental defences and the Guardian had reached out with his mind and stolen the information he needed. The Ecclesiarch instantly shielded his thoughts with impenetrable walls of defiance.

"You are not alone in your mastery of thought stealing Ecclesiarch Srisk."

His name sounded like a curse as the Guardian deliberately pronounced each syllable.

"I thought your kind extinct. How about that. That is one count of genocide that Faran' Mctal will have to erase from his list of victories. At least I will take pleasure in telling him."

Murac' Amor took a step closer.

"Your masters must want you dead? Why else would they send a Ventorian to meet the Moretti?"

"It wouldn't be the first time" shrugged the Ecclesiarch.

Srisk pumped the undercarriage on his rifle and the explosive projectile burst towards the Guardian. In a surprise move Murac' Amor rushed forward to meet the round bringing his empty arm in front of him as he did so. A circular power shield instantly shimmered into being and the large calibre round exploded against it. The blast reflected back off the shield throwing Srisk and the Thornbred from their feet.

Warning icons flashed on Srisk's HUD. He shook his head to clear his mind. His rifle was out of reach and the Guardian was seconds away with his hammer sparking. Srisk directed power into his outstretched gauntlet and magnetised it. The rifle vibrated and then snapped across the floor into the Ecclesiarch's hand. Srisk rolled just as the immense head of the maul smashed the rock where he had been. He squeezed the trigger and a salvo of shots peppered the Guardian's armour. Chunks of black Graphene and silver shards filled the air but the rounds did not penetrate Murac' Amor's flesh.

Srisk ran behind one of the pillars. He ducked as the crackling maul pulverised a section and the remaining column above it collapsed to the floor. The engulfing dust cloud gave the Ecclesiarch valuable seconds and he sprinted towards the chancel and then rolled out into the main aisle. Kneeling on one leg he took a deep breath and changed his view to infrared. He calmly squeezed the trigger repeatedly, executing each of the bemused Thornbred with a singular headshot. He needed to focus on the Guardian, the foot soldiers would hamper his efforts. He moved again as Murac' Amor crashed through two more supporting pillars and his hammer demolished a stone altar.

Srisk fired as he ran. Most rounds splintered armour, a couple found the joints and buried through Murac' Amor's flesh and organs. One sailed through the giant's mouth shattering a tooth before exiting through his cheek. They did not even slow the hulking Guardian. As the last slug left the smoking barrel of his whisper rifle Srisk slid the weapon across the floor and grabbed his sword.

A chunk of flying masonry thumped into the Ecclesiarch knocking him out through the doors and skidding into the pool. Srisk scrambled backwards from the water as the long muscular arm of the Guardian reached for his legs. Murac' Amor could not fit through the opening but it wouldn't take him long to smash his way in. Srisk rolled to one side and then chopped down with his molecular blade. He was aiming for the wrist. Murac' Amor flinched back at the last moment and the sword cut a deep swathe in the stone floor. Srisk rolled again this time towards his opponent. He grabbed the belt from one of the dead Thornbred and removed a blister grenade. Running between the giant's legs he slapped the ordinance on the inside of the Guardian's shin. The explosion sent Srisk skidding up the aisle. More warnings filled his head-up display. A red twenty-five percent held his attention.

Murac' Amor turned slowly. He staggered on his injured leg. Brown blood gushed from the wound. He was far from finished. Srisk knew in a battle of attrition, he would lose. He needed to end this now. The Ecclesiarch ran headlong towards the Guardian. He ported the remaining power in his suit to the front chest plate and magnetised it. His Achilles servos vented and shot him from the floor. He held his sword firmly with both hands as the electro-magnetic field kicked in and pulled him into the metal chest plate of Murac' Amor. The magnetic pull slammed against the Guardian so quickly that the giant warrior could not stop it. Srisk's sword drove deep into the Moretti's core.

Murac' Amor roared in pain. He reached for the parasite on his chest and despite the magnetic lock ripped Srisk away. The Ecclesiarch held tightly to his sword and dragged it sideways as he was torn free. The fingers of the Guardian's power suit threatened to crush him. He had moments before he would be pulped. He changed the mode on the sword and electrical tendrils danced around the glowing blade. This was his last chance. Srisk stabbed the sword into the giant's wrist. The electrical fields of both combatants' power armour and the sword clashed and erupted in an apocalypse of light. The Guardian fell backwards releasing Srisk in the process. His armour had shorted out but so had Srisk's. The Ecclesiarch estimated he had approximately four seconds before Murac' Amor's suit rebooted. His own would take much longer, if it restarted at all.

Without the power servos and hydraulic rams the suit may as well have been a metal coffin. As always Srisk had calculated this outcome. He triggered his suit release and forced his aching body upwards. He dragged his arms free from the armoured carapace and stepped from the leg units. His back and chest plates fell to the floor as he ran. Srisk vaulted onto the prone body of the Guardian. He could hear the motors whine into life. His bare feet were ripped and torn as he ran across the pockmarked torso. He reached Murac' Amor's neck just as the giant's suit rebooted. Srisk fell to his knees. He rammed the molecular sword through the Guardian's voice box and severed the spinal cord.

Murac' Amor twitched once. Srisk sliced to the left and right and the cauterised head of the Guardian tumbled backwards. The Ecclesiarch breathed deeply. He was unused to the air against his skin, to movement without mechanics and with no feedback on his condition apart from the pain his body was relaying to his brain. He didn't enjoy the feeling.

Srisk walked slowly across the debris strewn floor to the motionless body of Lelani. She looked peaceful despite the covering of dust. He knelt beside her and took hold of her hand. Even without his suit he knew she was dead.

"Too many innocents" he muttered to himself. He folded her arms gently across her chest and closed her eyelids. "I am sorry."

*

It was a further three days before the small fighter took off from the ruined desert city. Srisk had been relieved to discover that some of the natives had survived the onslaught, hidden deep within the cavern complex. He helped them bury their dead and remove all traces of the vile

Moretti. The burnt remains of the bodies and supplies were scattered to the winds. Srisk explained that word of the Bone Devils must be erased from history. The frightened population did not understand but agreed to their hooded saviour's instructions.

Srisk knew the hardy race would rebuild. They would survive, but nothing would ever be the same for them again. FOUR policy would have decreed that any civilisation or part thereof that had endured a third-kind close encounter would be either inducted into the Federation or erased. Srisk wished neither upon the innocent world of Kalleeka. Only the Noxvata had answers as to why this happened.

The Apocris entered the Gee Seven gate with Sangelon as its destination.

*

The worlds of Sangelon had been shrouded from the Federation since the dawn of the Primes. It resided deep within the Soul Shift Arm of the galaxy. Far enough away to avoid prying eyes and linked to the rest of the known galaxy via the mysterious Ninth Gate. The gate itself was a well kept secret. All system gates were numbered and legend told that the ninth had been destroyed as a star had turned super-nova. The area was renamed the Ninth Cloud. That currently, the main gates leapt from eight to ten was an accepted fabrication by all but a chosen few. The Sangelon system was home to the Noxvata and they required complete secrecy.

Within the Ninth Cloud only one planet was habitable. It was originally called Tempus-Endromis. Over the vast stretches of time the world had lost its name, being referred to as Sangelon Prime by some until eventually it was now simply known as the same name as the star it orbited. Sangelon.

The home world of the Lords of the Balance was further shrouded by a celestial sandwich of a vast asteroid field and fiery nebula. It was the perfect hiding place.

The majority of the planet's surface was covered in volcanic activity. From space the planet gave off an orange hue as the glow from the lava fields reflected off the thin sulphuric atmosphere. Nothing was known of the indigenous population or even if there had been one. The inhospitable environment only made the violent world more suitable to the Noxvata's purposes.

Within such a volatile world, building a lasting habitation would have been difficult if not impossible. The Noxvata had overcome this by building a city that moved. Obscura was a city like no other. Constructed on a platform that was held aloft by four massive caterpillar tracks. The iron treads were themselves as tall as an average skyscraper and on this sat the black towers of Obscura. The airtight city derived an endless source of power from the planet core, from which colossal thermal generators provided drive to the mammoth tracks and electricity for those who lived above. It moved so slowly that only time lapse photography would have revealed any motion. The other giveaway would have been the craterous indentations left behind by the gargantuan machine.

The tectonic plates were constantly monitored so that the city could be moved to a safe area in the event of an eruption or earthquake. In the unlikely situation of an unpredicted magmatic event the city had another trick. On each corner of the moving platform resided a massive cylindrical tower. They were not living quarters but giant turbine jets. They were capable of lifting the city to safety. That had happened only once in the last thousand years.

There were few in the Federation that knew of the city's existence, fewer still that had ever seen it. The vast majority of traffic into the Obscura were the Warriors of the Balance that served the Noxvata or the occasional supply craft. To see a Federation cruiser approach the crawling leviathan was an unusual if not a unique occurrence. A sleek white craft marked with the royal household of Keterus-Alpha was given permission to dock.

All dealings with the Lords of the Balance were conducted within the Inner Sanctum. The grand chancel was a shameless expression of power. Every cornice, pillar, plinth or recess was carved or contained gilt statues. The skill of the artisans that had created it was unparalleled. It was a masterpiece. Ironic that so very few ever witnessed its dark beauty. As exceptional as it was, all of it was constructed using a mixture of black basalt and black-steel, which made it intentionally overbearing and foreboding.

The tall woman dressed in a flowing scarlet gown felt no such awe. She had been here before. She was born to the royal household of Keterus-Alpha. Her feelings would never be betrayed by her demeanour.

She stood in front of five tall black monoliths. These represented the Lords of Balance. The Noxvata would never appear in person. If indeed they were humanoid entities at all. Three of the smooth stone slabs glowed and faint facial features could be made out. The central stone spoke.

"All is in hand Baroness. Our envoy returns forthwith."

Rainah was secretly pleased that they had used her official title. Nothing was certain when dealing with the Noxvata. That they had done her the courtesy of a proper address was a good sign. The Baroness twisted her head to look over her shoulder as she heard a heavy footfall. She watched the tall hooded figure approach and then bent to one knee in front of the monoliths.

"Baroness Rainah, this is one of our oldest bondsmen, Ecclesiarch Srisk. Srisk, this is Baroness Rainah from the royal house of Keterus-Alpha."

Srisk bowed towards the long haired woman. He returned his gaze to the glowing slab that now addressed him.

"We have warned you before about entering the Sanctum armed."

"My apologies Lords. My memory is deteriorating with age."

"We will discuss it later." Another of the stones glowed with the comment. It was the central monolith. Of them all, Srisk despised that one the most. "What of your latest charge? You look empty handed. Please do not tell us you have failed in your mission once again?"

"Of sorts" confessed Srisk.

"Explain yourself!" The stone shook.

Srisk looked towards the Baroness.

"Should the lady hear my report?"

"She is privy to this mission. Please continue Ecclesiarch." The instruction came from the left hand obelisk. Srisk was convinced it was a female entity.

"I met with the Guardian as instructed. However he was not conducive to travelling. Especially when he became aware of the size of his cabin. We exchanged words and the Moretti Guardian Murac' Amor and his retinue left for Dark Space."

"Really?" It was the central monolith again. "You expect us to believe that you, a Ventorian of all people, met with a Moretti and both parties walked away unharmed?"

"Yes my Lord. I have mellowed over time. My past remains in the past" replied Srisk.

"And your suit's recall log will verify this?"

Srisk had already had Liktus reprogram the recording that he took whilst planet-side.

"It is slightly damaged, but yes, I believe it will."

"This is not good enough." It was the Baroness that interrupted. "What of our agreement?"

"You will have what we promised Baroness Rainah. On occasions, plans must be changed. We will deal with your brother. Now you must excuse us as the less you know, the better."

Rainah scowled at the hooded warrior and flicked her hair in protest as she stormed past him and strode out of the chancel. Srisk waited until the he heard the clunk of the Sanctum doors closing.

"We are dealing directly with the Federation now?" he asked.

"To whom we address and what we choose to say is of no concern to you" came the reply.

Srisk glared from under his cowl.

"This is not the first time you have failed in your mission Ecclesiarch."

"I accept that" agreed Srisk. "Perhaps I should retire?"

"We all know that is not an option."

"Service until my death?" suggested Srisk.

There was a moment's silence.

"We have decided that you require a crew. Perhaps with more hands you may once again become a valuable resource. We understand you already have a pilot."

Srisk could sense the veiled threat. He had refused to lead a team on several occasions. He knew now that was no longer a path he could tread. He bowed his head slightly.

"As you wish"

"We have selected three worthy candidates. The data will be transferred to the Apocris. You have four lunar weeks to assemble the team."

"And then what would you have us do?" asked Srisk.

"We are indebted to the Baroness. You and your team will solve her current problem regarding her brother."

"Her brother?"

"Baron Valah."

"And what would you like us to do to him?"

"Bring him here. Your presence on Keterus-Alpha must not be discovered, and Ecclesiarch, he must be alive."

"He is just one man. I am sure that will not be a problem."

The left stone glowed.

"I am sure that has been said on more than one occasion about you Ecclesiarch. Do not underestimate the Baron. The royal households of the Cursus system have not remained in power due to bloodline alone. Valah will not be an easy target."

Srisk bowed again.

"As you command." Srisk turned to leave, but the central monolith lit up.

"Do not fail this task Ecclesiarch. We have tolerated your failure for long enough. I hope we understand each other?"

Srisk walked away.

"Perfectly" he whispered to himself.

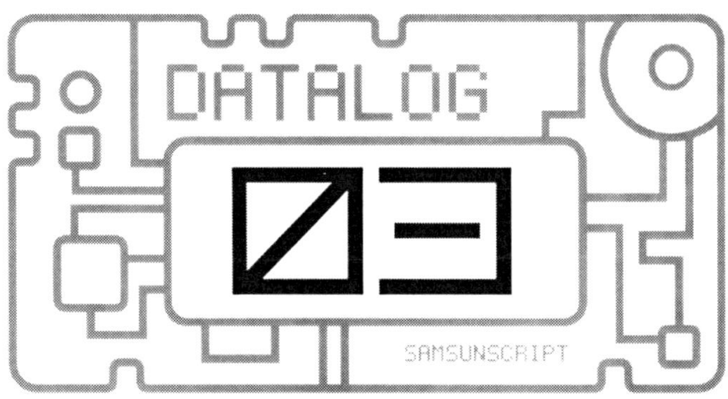

Soul-Warden

The stench of the proterium mines wafted up to her lofty position. Fortunately her vented mask removed the majority of the smell, but the odour was so overpowering some of it still seeped in. It was why anyone venturing outside of the air locked mining colony wore a full hazardous environment suit. Not Seelia. They were far too cumbersome plus the bright yellow just wasn't her colour, and she would have stood out like a rescue beacon. Her cyber-physiology had been engineered to cope with hazardous chemicals so it wouldn't harm her. It was just unpleasant.

She blocked out the constant din of the drilling with her headphones. Not that she ever took them off, even if there wasn't any background noise. Seelia was born and bred on Molva Prime. A small planet in the Corevose System. Its size was the main problem. Molva was an advanced society but the population exploded as its citizens lived longer and most diseases had been genetically erased. Whilst this was a positive change, the lack of space to live, work and for recreation was soon swallowed up. Countless generations had shaped the world of Molva and for those who didn't know, they could have easily mistaken the entire planet as a man-made entity.

In the early expansion years the trend was to extend beneath the surface, but as technology improved the habitations stretched up into the sky. The face of Molva was not the only thing to evolve. As the population leapt from six billion to over seventy-two billion, civilisation and social structure evolved. The major change came from overcrowding. Personal space became the one thing every person sought and held sacred. All interactions devolved to an electronic form. Speech stopped. Intimacy faded. The civilisation of Molva turned into a collection of seventy-two billion individuals. They neither liked, or needed interaction.

Seelia's current profession as a collector suited her unsociable upbringing. She worked alone, usually in isolated locations. When she did have to communicate with other beings it was under her terms and for the shortest time possible.

A constant stream of Tovan Electro-Synth poured through her sound cancelling headphones and she gently tapped her feet to the beat. The music suddenly stopped. A message alert sounded and an icon appeared on the thin blue eye shield that arced between each ear housing. Seelia looked at the icon and blinked. The message opened.

[Is it done?]

Seelia thought about not replying, but then changed her mind. She tilted her forearm and her fingers tapped on the keypad control that was strapped around her wrist.

[No] she replied.

She swiped across the control pad and accessed her communications menu. She tabbed down and selected - External Comms. Off.

She pulled her legs up to her chest and flicked a quick glance at the clock on her visor. Six twenty. Not long now she thought.

She looked down. Everything looked so peaceful. Even the belchers chugging out thick grey smoke and the extractors sporadically venting gas were somehow relaxing to her. She knew what lay inside the sprawling silver buildings. People. This was just one of the many mining colonies in the Rodo Field. Even out here in the Nelith System, light years from any Prime worlds there were people. The Rodo Field was a vast area of planetary debris that had collected since the birth of the galaxy. Some rocks were only hundreds of metres across others like the one Seelia was on, could be classified as a dwarf planet. They all had one thing in common - Proterium. The main material used in fusion reactors. It had been mined in the Rodo Field for seven hundred years and there was enough to last for another seven hundred.

Seelia felt a slight vibration in the smoke stack she was leaning against. She was atop one of the three giant vents that poured the pollutants from the colony into space. The gravitational pull of the dwarf planet was weak so most escaped into deep space, but anyone who had ever ventured outside the safety of the mining catacombs, would have seen the thick layer of chemical waste that covered everything. She checked that her magnetic anchor was secure. It was. The metal tube rattled and hissed as unknown pathogens pumped high into the atmosphere.

One more glance at the time. Six twenty-five.

She reached to her back and unhitched the rifle. Laying it across her legs she unfolded the barrel and then the stock. Once it had clicked into placed she extended it slightly and then checked the magazine was firmly in place. She looked at her visor menu. The system tracked her retina. She selected: External device. Then scrolled down and blinked as the entry - Maizon GB Sniper, appeared. A flashing icon signalled a connection and she ran a diagnostic on the gun. Everything was in order. Seelia flicked her long white hair back over her shoulder and looked down the sight. She zoomed in and out and satisfied with her test she made her way around the thin walkway and lay down in the position she had already marked out. Once again she adjusted the zoom. This time she focused on her target.

Far across the other side of the colony near the docking zone was one of the few places those inside had a good view over the mining complex. It was a viewing walkway that linked the arrivals lounge to the main hub. It was a glass tube ringed with titanium bands every metre. It had been originally designed to give those arriving a welcoming view of their new home. The authorities would have replaced it years ago if cost had allowed, as now it gave a realistic snapshot of how grim and grey the Rodo Field could be.

Seelia twisted the dial on top of the scope as wind and gravitational readings filed down on her data-slate. She watched as the nine blinked and turned to a zero. Calm flooded her body. Her breathing relaxed as she watched the three men enter the walkway.

She cursed into her respirator. One of the two bodyguards was blocking her shot. She had ten metres. He wasn't going to move. Seelia brushed the sensitive trigger to its first position and an optical stamp pin pointed the temple of the bodyguard. She squeezed the trigger and the magnesium round left the chamber. She drew breath and turned up the volume on her music. In the distance the bullet had to travel, the guard would have moved slightly but the tracker within the round was locked to the optical targeting point and the bullet adjusted accordingly. It punched a neat hole in the glass before it opened up and obliterated the bodyguard's head. Panic ensued. Seelia's target doubled over spewing the contents of his stomach onto the floor. The second bodyguard reacted well and made to cover his charge. He turned for a moment and was about to give instructions to run for cover when a second shot thudded into his chest and blew his heart and lungs out of his back.

Seelia looked through her scope. Her target stood completely still. Fear had rooted him to the spot. People were running behind him screaming yet he was oblivious to everything. She zoomed in closer. She could see the desperation in his eyes. She pulled the trigger. He was just another person. She hated people.

Seelia opened her console and typed.

[Done. Meet in ten. Have payment ready]

She had abseiled to the bottom of the tall chimney stack before the reply blipped in.

[Ogia Lounge. Don't be late]

She acknowledge the message and then cut her comms. Seelia ran across the roof of the building which housed the drop shafts and then slid down to the surface. She tapped the code into the panel on the airlock and to her relief it slid open. She repeated the process once inside and this time had to wait as cleaning gas poured into the chamber. As the green 'All Clear' light illuminated she stepped into the interior of the mining colony. Wrapping her rifle in her cloak she threw it up and over the myriad of pipes that connected and supplied every part of the complex.

She walked calmly through the brightly lit corridors keeping her head down staring only at the metal walkway in front of her. Although she would never have understood or wanted to admit it, Seelia would be considered beautiful by most bipedal humanoid races. In her line of work she wanted the least amount of attention possible which was even more acute due to her genetics. As it was, her silver skin, her crystal blue eyes, long white hair and tall slender figure made her stand out from the crowd. She increased her pace and pushed her way through into one of the precincts.

These places were her worst nightmare. Full of people. Eating, drinking, shopping and enjoying themselves. There were two precincts in this particular colony. Each one provided various recreational pleasures that would suit the tastes of most genus types. If there was something worse than the toxic waste that was being pumped into the atmosphere then Seelia considered this to be it. She rode the lev-steps to the lower level and made her way past the numerous cafes, bars and clubs. She stopped and looked up. The holographic sign overhead read: The Ogia Lounge. The scripted text flowed through a star shape that rippled through the colour spectrum. Seelia pushed opened the door and walked inside.

The vast majority of the population throughout the Rodo Field were from the closest habitable planet of Celadus. They were hardy, dedicated and reliable workers but like all races there were exceptions. Apart from the Celadians, a handful of other alien races sought work, refuge or solace in the sprawling mining community.

Seelia slid into a booth opposite a Celadian exception. Coden Rastner was typical of his race in physical looks; dark brown pitted skin, square set jaw, orange eyes, a bulky frame with three finger hands finishing his muscular arms. That was all he had in common with his hardworking, honest brethren. He wore a wide brimmed hat which kept the top half of his face in shadow. Over discreet body armour he wore a long leather coat that was decorated by brands. He reminded Seelia of a Cull Wrangler from her home world.

Coden had left the reputable role of a miner to pursue a darker profession. He ran the underground betting syndicate, provided an unofficial solution service and also organised the import of banned substances into the Rodo Field. He was a scoundrel and drug dealer.

Coden had operated in the colony for more than fifteen years. He had managed such a long reign by paying off the Magister and avoiding the authorities by using hired help such as Seelia for the more sordid jobs. The remoteness of the Rodo Field helped keep his activities hidden. Everything had been moving smoothly until the Magister had refused to sign-off on Coden's latest shipment request. Seelia had no idea what the contraband was, but it must have been something highly illegal if the Magister had got cold feet. Coden's simple solution was to remove the person stopping him from achieving his goal. He sat, chewing on Kalia plant extract, with no comprehension of the repercussions his actions would cause. With the current Magister removed it would be months before a replacement was appointed. As far as Coden was concerned, all but one of the obstacles in the way of his plans had been addressed. He was about to take care of the last.

"Great job, although a tad messy. I did actually only pay you to take out the Magister and not both of his bodyguards. I hope you won't be increasing your price because of it?" Coden's tone was almost jovial. He had obviously taken some of his own narcotic product.

Seelia typed on her keypad. Coden's Life-log bleeped. He read the message.

[No]

"I heard about your people. Never thought it was true. Even sat opposite me now you still won't talk to me?"

Bleep. Bleep.

[No] [Payment?]

"Yes about that. I wanted to see if there was room for re-negotiation?" Coden nodded towards two burly looking miners. One slid in next to Seelia and the other sat next to Coden. "What do you say? Forgive the pun" Coden and his lackeys laughed.

Bleep.

[No]

"Is this starting to annoy you?" Coden was talking to his two colleagues. They both nodded in agreement. Coden reached across the table and grabbed Seelia around the throat. "Look you silver witch, this is my offer. I'll pay you half of what we agreed as I'm not a complete thief. I think that's only fair after the mess you made. This place will be crawling with 'Fleas' because of you. I suggest you take it or we'll make a mess of our own."

Seelia twisted her head slightly. She tapped away on her keypad ignoring the three fingers around her neck. Coden's Life-log vibrated across the table. He released his hold and picked up his device.

[My counter-offer: Double the money we agreed as no one touches me without my permission. Transfer the money within fifteen seconds or this will be your last day in this backwater hellhole]

Anger spread quickly across Coden's face and he lunged across the table trying to punch Seelia. She moved just enough so that his fist sailed by her headphones and then with one hand chopped down on Coden's elbow joint forcing him to hit the table. Her other arm shot out, and as it did so a long slender blade sprang out over the back of her fist. The thin weapon punched straight through Coden's eye and into his brain. She withdrew the blade and sliced in an arc towards the henchman next to her. The razor sharp point carved through his throat and dark blue blood fountained into the air. The other sidekick had drawn a lath-pistol and was about to pull the trigger.

Seelia slid beneath the table just as a molten hot bolt blew the back of the booth to pieces. She rammed the deadly blade into the legs of the remaining Celadian, and as she scurried out from under the table, ripped the knife across his belly disembowelling him. The dying minder managed to discharge a final shot which smashed into the ceiling. Debris clattered down over the bloody scene. Seelia looked around. All eyes were upon her. The club owner had already raised the alarm. The compulsory metal shutters were already closing. She ran for the door and rolled under the barricade before it slammed into the floor. Outside people had already scattered. Running scared after they had heard the first gunshot. Even in this remote place it wouldn't be long before the authorities arrived. Seelia needed a way out. As she heard the final security shutters all around the precinct clatter into place, she knew that was going to be a problem.

The word of law varied across the Shakari galaxy. FOUR had established the idea of a galactic police force that could operate across the star systems and that all member planets would contribute towards a set of generic laws that would apply regardless of race or creed. It started off as a simple concept but had evolved into a complex organisation that now operated as a formidable independent entity. In simple terms all of the various arms operated under the Federation Law Enforcement Agency. That had given rise to the slang term 'Flea' to describe all law enforcement personnel. The agency had three main arms:

- The White Mission. Known as 'Ghosts'. By far the most numerous they are stationed throughout the galaxy and dealt mostly with civilian issues.
- The Unity Order. Known as 'Ghouls'. Highly trained operatives that had the unpopular task of policing the huge ranks of all star systems' armed forces.
- The Soul-Wardens. Known as 'Wraiths'. The elite of the Agency. Granted unique powers of inquisition and had powers of judge, jury and executioner. Often ruled over political, global or inter-system quarrels.

Even in this far flung outpost there was a posting of The White Mission. As with most positions of power, they had stretched their remit, and laws and edicts not necessarily sanctioned by the Agency had found their way into the mining community. Normally limited to policing minor quarrels or turning a paid blind eye to the occasional illegal shipment they had been woken from their stupor by the Magister's assassination. The precinct alarm meant only one thing to them. Further trouble.

Seelia was unarmed apart from her wrist blade. That would be little use against a Ghost's assault cannon. When the shutters had gone down most of the population had been detained within each precinct outlet. There were a handful that had been trapped in the main access ring. There weren't enough for Seelia to lose herself in a crowd. She leapt up the lev-steps onto the first floor. Shouts came from across the mall. She turned to see the white uniform of a Ghost about to check the security footage of a shuttered establishment. The flick of her long snowy hair caught his eye. He raised his hand to his Recit and called out.

"Hold there!"

Seelia jumped to the translucent lev-step above her head. A large calibre round smashed the glass barrier where she had been stood. Seelia pulled herself up and sprinted up the bouncing steps towards the third level. Splintered glass and metal chased at her heels as the chasing Ghost let rip with a violent salvo.

She reached the hard floor of level three and skidded directly into the feet of another Ghost. He levelled his rifle but Seelia moved with lightning speed between his legs and standing up behind him wrapped her forearm under his helmeted chin and pulled his head back. With a swift blow she punched her fist blade into his temple. She was about to retrieve his rifle when heavy shots pulped into the dead Ghost's body sending them both skidding backwards. Seelia flipped the body and ran to the balcony edge. She leapt onto the balustrade and then jumped up. Her fingers found the lip of the next level and she pulled herself up just as rounds punched fist sized holes in the plazcrete. Shrapnel from the gunfire pockmarked her legs. Ignoring the pain she flipped over the glass barrier. She focussed on her visor and selected: Trouble Playlist. Then she increased the volume.

Seelia grabbed a waste-compactor and kicked it violently managing to rip it from its moorings. She returned to the lev-steps and hurled the metal can at the Ghost's legs. It barrelled him from the narrow glass platform and he tumbled downwards. Ignoring the shots whistling past her head she vaulted to meet the other White Mission guard. She flew into him with her knee cracking his mirrored visor. Seelia stamped down on his rifle which caused the Ghost to lean over and reveal a gap between his helmet and chest armour. Seelia repeatedly stabbed the thin blade into the opening. Blood gushed from the wound. She grabbed the rifle and kicked the spluttering guard out into the precinct atrium. She looked down to see the other Ghost regain his footing. She flicked the auto switch on the assault rifle and opened fire. The White Mission officer was vaporised in a hail storm of steel.

Seelia was about to run when she saw movement over her shoulder. Before she could turn she felt the barbs pierce her back and then the crack of electricity filled the air. Her body spasmed under the shock and Seelia lost consciousness.

*

The bright white light of the confined cell burnt into her retinas, even with her eyes closed. It was nothing compared to the offensive onslaught on the rest of her senses. Seelia had been stripped of her equipment and left in just her under garments. Her silver skin was blackened by bruises. Dried blood coated her face and matted her once white hair. She reached to cover her ears and drew her feet to her chest.

There was no way out of this situation. Part of her knew that this was always a likely future, although she had hoped to delay for a few years at least.

The white wall ahead shimmered and suddenly became transparent. A stern looking Ghost stared in at her. He pressed his hand against the glass and a red light illuminated.

"I'm glad to see you are finally awake. I've never seen anything like you before. A Molvian assassin of all things. It seems that you are a wanted person. A possible twenty-seven murders, plus the undisputed killing of my three White Mission brothers. Do you have anything to say before we start your interrogation."

Seelia didn't move. 'Twenty-seven'. She smiled to herself. Add two hundred to that total and that might come close. The Ghost continued.

"You know the penalty you face. You will be recycled. We'll get a good price for those eyes, and maybe the legs if they remain in that condition."

Still Seelia remained motionless.

"Look, we both know how this ends. You're a high value catch. A Soul-Warden will be here within days. He will break your mind. If you can tell me what I need to know, give me names and places I can make your short time with us as comfortable as possible. What do you say?"

Seelia looked up. She swung her legs from the bench and walked to the clear glass separation shield. She stared directly into his orange eyes. Seelia huffed on the glass and then wrote in the mist 'GFY'. The Ghost held her gaze. His Recit crackled and he touched his hand to his earpiece.

"What do you mean, here? How can he be here already? I'm on my way."

She watched as he walked away without another word. The glass turned opaque, and Seelia returned to the bench and drew her legs up to her chest. She closed her eyes and tried to gather her strength. Her conscience nagged at her. Why bother? It is all futile. This is the end for you. She conceded. Her life was over.

She had withdrawn so completely that she did not notice the white wall once again lose its colour. It was only the metallic tap against the clear glass that grabbed her attention. She looked up at the tall figure on the other side. Fear touched her soul. She had heard tales about the Soul-Wardens and the cloaked individual that engulfed the security screen embodied every terrible detail she had conjured in her mind.

"Do you want to live?" He asked. There was zero emotion in his voice.

Seelia nodded weakly.

"That is a good start. Will you connect with me?"

Seelia was apprehensive. Why would he ask? He could reach in to her mind and take whatever he wanted. What kind of tactic was he employing? She looking into his glowing eyes and opened her thoughts.

<What have I got to lose?>

<Your life> came the reply.

<Do not toy with me. I know that my life is forfeit. Whatever it is you want take it and then do what you must.>

<You are a fatalist. Interesting. I am not who you think I am, Seelia of Molva. Tell me. Have you ever heard of the Lords of the Balance?>

Seelia stood up and walked to the glass.

<They are a myth>

<They are many things, but a myth is not one of them. I am one of their representatives.>

<You are not a Soul-Warden?>

<The local Mission believe that I am.>

<Then who are you and why are you here?>

The tall character turned and picked up a small cargo pod. He tapped the security screen and it shimmered briefly before vanishing. He handed the box to Seelia.

<These are your belongings I believe?>

Seelia took the cargo pod.

<Thank you, but you haven't answered my question.>

<I will explain as you get ready.>

Seelia took her gear to the bench with a sense of trepidation. She clamped her headphones over her ears and instantly she felt better.

<My name is Ecclesiarch Srisk. I am an envoy for the Lords of the Balance. You have been chosen to join our fold. >

Seelia finished strapping on her wrist equipment.

<What is the catch? What if I say no?>

<You and I both know you won't refuse. As for your alternative? Well I think you were already starting to come to terms with that life-path. I do not know what the future holds for you. It is a time of change for myself also. I will be honest and admit that I do not want the responsibility for someone else, but in these times of uncertainty maybe an alliance of adversity will benefit all concerned.>

<How do I know you are for real? This could just be a con orchestrated by the Ghosts>

<What if it were? It would still provide you with more opportunity than you had before I arrived.>

Seelia conceded the point.

<What is it you want me to do?>

<I am in the process of assembling a team. You were the first on my list. There are two more.>

<What then?>

<Then> Srisk paused for a moment. <Then I would imagine your unique skill set will be required.>

<Of course, but once we're out of here, what's to stop me running. Please don't misunderstand, if you're genuine then I'm grateful for the free ticket out of here, but 'Lords of the Balance' and all that - shouldn't you be selling me a higher purpose or something?>

Something akin to laughter chortled from beneath Srisk's hood.

<Would that work?>

Seelia raised her eyebrows.

<I didn't think so. Besides I would be the wrong person to preach the virtues of our organisation. I am here because I must be. You will make your own choices and the hand of fate will either embrace you or destroy you.>

Seelia finished lacing her long shin length boots and looked up at the Ecclesiarch.

<If we're going to shoot our way out of here I'll need a weapon.>

<The Warriors of the Balance are not immune to the powers of the Agency. Killing members of the White Mission would bring unnecessary attention.>

<Then how do you intend we leave? Are we just going to walk out?>

<Yes. That was my plan.> Srisk threw a set of binding cuffs in Seelia's direction. <Put those on.>

Seelia clamped the cuffs on each wrist.

<You realise this is not the best way to start a relationship?>

Srisk placed a metal gauntlet on her slender shoulder.

<If you realised what lay ahead. Then maybe you would have chosen to stay.>

<Now you tell me?> Seelia smiled for the first time in her adult life.

City of the Lost

Volcanus. The largest and arguably one of the oldest Prime worlds in the galaxy. Orbiting the equally massive Hoid, a star that was approaching the end of its main sequence. The huge planet was home to the Volcanux, one of the founding races of FOUR.

The surface of Volcanus was a juxtaposition of both natural and constructed wonders. A myriad of record breaking buildings occupied the environment with an equally diverse and chart topping list of biological marvels. The vast cities continued the diversity with ancient monuments sitting side by side with modern metal and glass towers that reached out into space. Unique gravitational effects and undisclosed construction techniques made the major cities of Volcanus the only ones in the Shakari galaxy that transgressed their planet's atmosphere.

The contrasting environment was mirrored in the ruling companies that controlled Volcanus. A strong sense of morality and justice was aligned with misplaced principles and a willingness to overlook ethical issues if power, progress or money were involved. This gave the Noxvata many roads into the Volcanux civilisation.

*

Liktus guided the Apocris into the stellar dock with consummate skill. The spider arms of the docking platform stretched out in all directions and each was full with a variety of small to medium sized star craft. Larger ships loomed overhead, some anchored in stationary orbits some being manoeuvred into position by compact tugs. The lower dock was connected to one of the mesmerising towers that reached up from the planet surface. They had been created to allow for swift and easy trade. They had contributed to making Volcanus one of the richest planets in the galaxy.

Liktus leapt through the airlock and was swiftly on his way towards the arrival gate before Srisk called him back. The diminutive red creature had a small backpack slung over his shoulder. He stared up at the Ecclesiarch with his large glassy eyes.

"Please don't make me stay Master" he pleaded.

"As much as I would enjoy your company, Volcanus is no place for you my friend. As outwardly welcoming as they might seem, I fear the underlying prejudice towards creatures such as yourself would make this an unpleasant stay."

Liktus looked towards Seelia for moral support. She tapped on her keypad.

[You can take my place]

The red reptilian smiled and Srisk glared at the silver-skinned female.

"I have a feeling we may have to depart this world in a hurry. Your role is crucial my friend."

Liktus lowered his head and his backpack slumped to the ground.

"I know" he mumbled. "Stay in the ship."

The odd couple watched as Liktus shuffled slowly back towards the airlock. Srisk turned to Seelia.

"Have you left all weapons behind?"

She nodded.

"They will scan us at the gate. The Lords of the Balance have paved the way for our arrival but it would be foolish to attract unnecessary attention. I am still uncertain that they will let us pass with this."

Srisk lifted the circular disk he held in his hand.

Seelia reached out to him.

<What is it?>

"A remote collar."

<The guy we're after, his neck is that wide?>

The Ecclesiarch nodded.

<He's going to want to come with us right? I wouldn't want to be forcing someone whose neck is wider than my shoulders.>

"Let's hope so."

The pair made an uneventful passage through the security checks and onto the mag-lev. They stepped into the next available capsule. Srisk locked his magnetic boots to the floor whilst Seelia sat in one of the bucket seats. A sturdy harness folded down over her head. The gargantuan planet below filled the view through the hexagonal windows. Seelia tucked her head to her chest trying to avoid the gaze of the dozen or so other alien visitors. She felt Srisk's mind touch her.

<Hold on.>

<You've been here before?>

<Once. A long time ago.>

<I sense trepidation in your thoughts.>

<I am hoping they have forgotten my last visit.>

Seelia was about to reply when the brake clamps hissed and the transport pod suddenly sank. She grabbed the harness as the g-force lifted her internal organs and bile gathered in her throat. She looked up. Others were experiencing similar effects. Seelia steadied her breathing and stopped fighting the falling sensation. As they sped towards the surface she marvelled at the view.

<Amazing isn't it?> commented Srisk.

<I've never seen anything like it.>

Seelia was transfixed to the cold glass taking in the wonders of Volcanus. They were descending into the sprawling metropolis of Hoighen. The city had been a centre of galactic commerce since the inception of gate travel. Monumental silver and black buildings of every shape and size covered the ground. Scattered amongst them were colossal trees. Some of the vast canopies stretched up and over smaller skyscrapers. Hoighen was a marriage of the natural and artificial. The developers had taken great care to design the buildings and transport network around the ancient plants. They had realised a millennia ago that they were essential to continued life on the planet. Even with air-scrubbers, weather adjustment and solar shielding nothing was as efficient as the mammoth forests and swelling oceans.

The mag-lev slowed as it neared a ninety degree curve and still the amazing sights kept flooding in.

Alongside the elevated rail was a huge lake. Its bright blue waters reflected the unusual collection of buildings that stood around its edge. Some were constructed from plazcrete moulded into fantastic shapes, resembling sculptures from an art gallery. Others were built from glowing metals and vast slabs of mirrored glass producing never-ending illusions of depth. Interspersed among these modern masterpieces were ancient stone buildings. Huge columns supporting domes and pitched roofs, carved statues and fascias coated every visible space. The trophy of the older buildings was a castle type structure that jutted out into the lake. It was monstrous. The giant slab-like towers at each corner leant in towards a central keep that rivalled some of the modern skyscrapers in height. It was a marvel now, let alone when it had first been constructed.

The most jaw-dropping of all the sights was located in the centre of the lake. It was a crashed star cruiser. It was partly submerged. Seelia turned from the window and looked at Srisk.

<What is that?>

<It's something we don't talk about> replied the Ecclesiarch.

Seelia stared into the darkness of his hood. Srisk conceded.

<It is the Vision of Antares. In its day it would have been the largest cruiser sailing the stars. It is a colony ship designed to carry half a million souls that would eventually populate another world. It crashed... in mysterious circumstances. Due to its fortunate landing place and the lack of casualties the authorities have left it as a monument and a symbol of the good fortune of Hoighen.>

<Don't tell me you had something to do with it?>

Seelia looked back out of the window at the astonishing sight. She turned again.

<Is that why you were reluctant to return? What happened Srisk?>

Seelia was excited. The Ecclesiarch dulled the mood.

<It is all a distant memory. We should be focussing on the task at hand.>

<Which is what exactly? You haven't told me anything other than his name. Ortig. Who is he? And more importantly why do we need that collar?>

<We are on our way to the Night Dome. It is home to broadcast studios of VNN. We are going to be live on the mainstream Volcanux entertainment network.>

<Television?>

<It is a reality show. Of sorts>

<You're joking, surely?>

<I'm afraid not. Our next prospective crew member will be appearing on this show. I don't believe he had much of a say in the matter. However it does mean we will be in front of the cameras also. The

Lords of the Balance have arranged it. Believe me Seelia of Molva, it is positively the last thing I want to be involved with.>

Seelia smiled at the Ecclesiarch's discomfort.

<What is the show called?>

<City of the Lost.>

*

The Night Dome like everything else on Volcanus was over sized. The black and white honeycomb structure stared at the sky like some prehistoric insect eye. It was home to one of the most popular shows on the Volcanus entertainment network. Once inside the reason for the voluminous span was clear. The dome housed an entire city. Twelve herculean pistons held the fabricated set aloft. Vertical stone walls stretched the entire perimeter and inside, the buildings mirrored the cities of the Western deserts. Square, flat roofed and closely packed. One built on top of another. Around the city stood a cobweb of gantries and walkways with enough cabling to stretch around the globe. Lighting fixtures, camera cranes and hoists finished the chaotic backdrop.

The top of the dome had been lit to reflect the sky outside. Just as in the real world the artificial light of day was being dimmed and false flickering stars started to appear against a black background.

Srisk and Seelia had been ushered to a wide platform that led out towards the reproduction city. Make-up artists had approached them trying to get them ready for camera. The guttural growl from Srisk was enough to send them running. A producer was now trying to explain the proceedings but the pair were consumed by their weapon choice. They were poring over a rack containing a diverse collection of primitive weapons. Srisk picked up a wide broadsword not too dissimilar to his molecular blade. He span it over in his hands before tapping the edge. Satisfied, he slung it over his back and it clanked as it mag-locked next to the circular collar he had been carrying earlier. Seelia picked up a crude looking pistol. She turned it over trying to ascertain how the ammunition was loaded. She looked up at the Ecclesiarch.

<Any idea how this works?>

<Forget it. You'll need something that won't run out of bullets.>

Seelia returned her focus to the rack and chose a slender but sturdy metal staff which tapered at each end.

Lights clacked into life and spotlights flicked across the gantry ahead. The stressed producer was still trying to grab Srisk's attention. Finally the big warrior looked down.

"What is it?"

"I was wondering if you could remove your cloak. Our viewers like to see the faces of all competitors. It will help you with your ratings, you know when it comes to voting, if they can identify with you."

"I think I will keep it" replied Srisk. "It will add to my mystery. I'm sure your viewers will appreciate the theatre."

The producer thought about it for a moment and whether he agreed or not he decided not to push the point.

"The show will start in ten. Once the city is lowered and the gate is opened the host will introduce you and that is your cue to move forward."

Srisk nodded his understanding.

<Are we really doing this?> Seelia sent the thought to the Ecclesiarch.

<Ortig will be entering the city from one of the other gates. We have to find him and persuade him to join us.>

<That doesn't sound so difficult.>

<That will be the easy bit. We then have to keep him and ourselves out of sight for three days until the city is lowered again.>

<Just exactly what is this show about?>

<It's best if you don't know>

Seelia's attention was torn as chains rattled and motors whirred and the large set descended. The prodigious hydraulic pistons supporting the platform slowly and smoothly lowered the city. Huge spotlights clanked open illuminating the metal gateway that was coming in to view. The fake city shook as it reached the bottom of its journey. A sliding bridge moved out towards the gates and a tall Volcanian jumped from a gantry and into the light.

"Friends! Welcome!"

He was exuberant and bursting with well practised excitement. He was a polished example of a Volcanian. Greyish-blue skin, piercing red eyes set under a protruding brow. Neat strips of tightly cropped hair stretched back over his head like a ploughed field. Scales covered his neck and faded out around his chin and tiny ears. He wore a red coat that split at the rear, over black trousers and plated knee length platform boots. His muscled torso was bare apart from a chunky necklace. A thin microphone was invisibly taped to his jaw line. He squared up to the nearest camera.

"I am Johan Vanderlos. You join me here on another exciting evening in the City of the Lost!"

Pre-recorded cheers and applause echoed around the set.

"What a week it was. I have to say I didn't see the vote swinging against the 'Mauler'. He has been a crowd favourite for weeks. Just when it looked like he might make it clear, you voted to spring the traps. How cruel you all are!"

Johan unveiled a perfect white smile for nearest the lens.

"They all know the risks. Let's get on with the show. Last night Burton Degalio escaped that evil den of iniquity - the one and only Scarlet Pike - What a great contestant he is, despite losing that leg he managed to make it to the gatehouse to trigger the escape vote."

Johan bounded towards the stained wooden gates.

"Remember voting is now closed. Burton's fate has been sealed. Let's open the gates and see what the Volcanian public has decided. Death or Glory?"

Johan let the question hang. It was then repeated over loudspeakers as a mindless chant. The volume increased as Johan worked the viewers into a frenzy.

"Open the gates!" he hollered.

The wooden doors creaked open to reveal a one-legged body hanging from the arch of the gatehouse. A canned 'Ahh' played out.

"Will anyone ever escape the City of the Lost? Let's meet our new competitors and find out. Please welcome Marin and Mascilla."

As the recorded applause rang out, Seelia tapped on her keyboard.

[Marin and Mascilla? Really?]

Srisk reached out with his mind.

<It's our fake names that you are concerned over?>

Suddenly they were both thrust into the spotlight and the perfumed host bounced to meet them.

"The City of the Lost lies ahead. It has been seven weeks since our last winner. How do you see your chances?"

Johan held a microphone in front of Seelia. She stared silently back at him. Srisk reached across.

"Let me answer that Johan. We are big fans of the show and have been training and studying hard. We think we have a strong chance."

"That's great!" replied Johan not listening to the answer. "Did you know that the Butcher of Merringrad is also entering the city this evening?"

"No I did not" lied Srisk.

"How do think you'll fare if you run into him?"

"I have a special gift for him."

"Interesting. So final question. What sets you apart from the rest of the opposition."

Srisk leaned into the nearest camera and held the microphone in front of his hooded face. He crushed the device and threw the bits into the air. At the same time he mustered a low timbre and said calmly.

"Because we are unpredictable."

Instructions fired from the director's headset and a loud cheer resounded. Johan had already leapt back onto the moving platform.

"Let's wish Marin and Mascilla luck. Remember you can follow all of their progress as well as vote on the City of the Lost, P.I.P. Now let's go to the South gate and meet our next contestant."

Seelia watched as the host soared upwards. The lights faded and the cameras briefly stopped rolling. Seelia saw Johan looking back towards her. He pointed two fingers at his eyes and then back at the Molvian assassin. Seelia flicked her fingers off both sides of her chin in the globally appreciated insult.

They walked towards the open gate.

<What was all that about? Have you lost your mind? Are you actually enjoying this nonsense.>

<We may need the public's support. It was an act. We are here for one reason only.>

<One last thing. Please tell me that Ortig is not the Butcher of Merringrad?>

Srisk was silent.

*

Johan had already gone through his routine for the opening of the South gate and the recorded jeers of the fake crowds indicated no dead bodies this time around. That didn't dampen the host's enthusiasm as he eagerly introduced the last entrant.

"You've all heard the stories. You know the dark depths of his depravity. Will he atone for sins within the city or will this become another massacre he adds to his long list? My friends , I am delighted to introduce to you, the one and only, Butcher of Merringrad."

Voluminous applause echoed throughout the studio and the spotlight moved from Johan to the black-steel box that was being pushed out onto the ramp.

The huge metal container had been custom made to hold the hulking figure that was clamped inside. Ortig was one of a kind. Literally. His home world of Calabris had long since been scoured clean as a wandering Neutron Star collided with the system. It had saved the Federation a job as the Calabrians were not accommodating its request for peace and unity. A handful of the natives escaped the collapse, and of these, most had been hunted and killed. Ortig was the last.

He was over eight feet tall and built like a giant ape. Huge, powerful shoulders with abnormally sized forearms. His head was squat, compact and hairless. Amber eyes shone under a ridged brow. Two long broken canine teeth poked down over his bottom lip. He wore only faded blue trousers that had been ripped, torn and stained. His dark blue skin looked and felt like stone, complete with fissures, cracks and chaotic marbling patterns running across it. As the spotlight flooded over him, his eyes intensified and he strained at the bonds that held him. He locked his gaze onto the posturing host who cautiously slid towards him. Johan held a microphone towards the captive.

"Welcome to the City of the Lost. Do you have any words for the viewers of Volcanus?"

Fury burned in Ortig's deep set eyes. He strained his neck forward and bit the top off the microphone. He spat it back into the face of Johan. The host leapt back. He rubbed his cheek where a wire mesh impression had been left. He angrily signalled for the attendants to usher the caged monster into the city. A make-up artist quickly powdered his face before once again Johan returned to the camera.

"What a character! I'm sure you're all as excited as I am to see what happens once he is released into the city. Keep watching and don't forget to vote. We'll be right back after these messages from our sponsors."

As soon as the camera light flicked off, Johan ranted at the director who was clearly not listening. He was watching as the containment unit was being pushed inside the gate. One of the attendants pressed a series of buttons on a hand-held remote. He looked around worriedly.

"What's the problem?"

"The release is not working."

"Then go and open it manually" shouted the Director.

"What if he gets loose?"

"Press the release catch and then run. We'll close the doors as soon as you're through."

The attendant looked reluctant to move.

"Do it now or lose your job" barked the Director.

They watched as the grey skinned Volcanian walked to the metal case. He lent around to access the manual release. Suddenly his body jerked and then staggered back minus his head.

"Shut the gates!" ordered Johan. "Raise the damn platform."

A deafening roar came from the city and the broadcast crew watched in shock and horror as the attendants head came soaring over the gatehouse towards them.

"This is going to be one hell of a show" smiled Johan.

*

Srisk and Seelia ignored the noise as the other competitors were given their introductions and the exuberant Johan wound up the opening of the show. They were crouched down behind the closed gate.

[So what's the deal?] The message tripped down on Srisk's feed.

"This is no ordinary game show, but you have probably gathered that already. The authorities use this place as a convenient way to get rid of unwanted prisoners, political activists and generally anyone they don't want to process through the court. As far as I understand, the whole city is full of nefarious types, that prefer its confines to that of a penal colony. It's also full of traps that, if caught, the Volcanian public can vote on. Any questions before we get started?"

<One. Why is Ortig called The Butcher?>

Seelia could feel the tension in his thoughts.

<I am sure he has killed a few people in his time, but then so have we. I am positive it is just spin by the entertainment company to make him into some sort of viewing sensation.>

<And that collar - what does it do exactly?>

<As Liktus explained it to me, apparently it emits a low frequency pulse that dulls the wearer's neuron receptors.>

Seelia raised her eyebrows.

<It makes him docile.>

<These are going to be a long three days.>

Srisk scanned the track ahead. The buildings on either side rose up four storeys high. The walls were flat with no windows or openings. It was an obvious funnel into whatever the show organisers had planned. His readings couldn't detect anything but it didn't feel right to the Ecclesiarch. He sidled past Seelia and placed his back against the wall. He cupped his hands and held them low enough for a foothold.

"Time to take a ride."

Without hesitation Seelia placed her foot onto the metal gauntlets. Srisk's suit whined as he powered his arms aloft sending Seelia flying into the air. She was so light that she easily cleared the roof of the building and disappeared over the top. Moments later she reappeared. She was about to ask how he intended to join her as there was no way she could lift his armoured bulk. She watched as Srisk punched a hole into the sandy covered wall. He then drew himself up and thrust the angular point of his boots into the stone. He repeated the process and was soon hauling himself onto the flat roof. Rubble tumbled from the holes he had made, down into the street.

From the lofty vantage point he could see a lot more but the city buildings were almost identical which made it almost impossible to discern a direction of travel. He had no idea from which gate Ortig would have entered.

<We'll head to the centre>

Srisk took one step across the flat roof and the structure creaked under his weight. An instant later the Ecclesiarch vanished in a cloud of dust.

His suit absorbed the landing and he remained upright. He cycled his ocular HUD to infrared to reveal the outlines of four beings. One rushed towards him with his arm over his head. Srisk raised his hand and a metal chink sounded as the attacker's sabre clattered against the Ecclesiarch's exoskeleton. Srisk thrust out with his other arm. The piston powered punch shattered the aggressor's ribcage and pulped his internal organs. Srisk reached over his shoulder grabbing the hilt of the crude sword. Swinging it low, he span three hundred and sixty degrees. Howls of pain filled the room as the remaining three tumbled into the darkness. The sword's edge was dull but the force that Srisk exerted was more than enough to cleave limbs. As Seelia dropped into the room Srisk had already twisted the neck of one screaming victim and now held another in his outstretched gauntlet.

"Where can I find Moreallis?" asked Srisk

The Volcanian grimaced his refusal to talk. Srisk snapped his neck. He discarded the body and walked to the last attacker. Both of his legs were missing at the shin and warm blood pumped from the wounds. He was going into shock. Srisk knelt by his side.

"Moreallis?"

"South and second" he murmured.

"How do you know what street is what, there are no signs"

"Ultra.." he gurgled. Srisk grabbed his head and lifted him upwards. "Ultraviolet."

Srisk released his grip and the Volcanian's head slapped back against the floor. He turned to Seelia.

"You'll be my eyes in the sky. Do you have a mode setting on your eye shield?"

Seelia nodded.

"Good. I'll get to the street, you can guide me."

*

Ortig ripped the last retaining bolt from its mooring and stepped into the dusty street. Lights inset high up in the building walls illuminated one by one like a runway start up sequence. They lit the street ahead.

Ortig strode directly down the middle of the road. He made four strides before a loud click sounded underfoot as he triggered a pressure plate. Shutters either side of him slid open revealing a panel full of holes. In a sudden rush of air hundreds of barbed spikes shot out of the trap. Ortig looked down as they harmlessly bounced off his skin and clattered to the floor. He picked up one of the projectiles and used it to remove an annoying piece of meat that was wedged between his teeth.

Ortig swung his head as several shadowy figures ambled into the street ahead. They were all armed with bolt weapons. The huge creature turned to his side and lowered his head like a battering ram and with bullets ricocheting off his impenetrable hide he smashed through the nearest wall.

The assembled group at the end of the street looked at each other in confusion as the sound of tumbling mortar and collapsing walls rumbled throughout the buildings. Suddenly the nearest fighter was buried in an explosion of stone as Ortig burst through next to them. His massive fist hammered down on top of the adjacent soldier. The momentum shattered his skull and forced his spine to buckle and pierce the skin on his back. The last Volcanian opened up his bolt gun at point blank range. To his shock the bullets just bounced off. Ortig ripped the weapon from the stunned fighter's hands and then clubbed him to death with it. Ortig thumped his chest and roared his arrival into the City of the Lost.

*

Srisk walked carefully, as close to the edge of the wide street as he could. Seelia leapt across the rooftops following the Ecclesiarch. With her visor set to ultraviolet she could clearly see the street numbering etched high on the walls. She tapped quickly into her keypad.

[Two figures. Recess. On your left. Twenty yards.]

She watched as Srisk turned into the alcove and impaled one of the forms. The other tried to fire a pistol, but the Ecclesiarch was too fast and pinned his hand. The struggling assassin pulled the trigger and a plasma bolt blew the end of his own boot off. Srisk reversed his grip snapping the screaming man's wrist. Grabbing the gun he shoved it under the assassin's chin and squeezed. Bone and brain decorated the wall.

Srisk's feed scrolled.

[Five more. Armed. Corner of South and tenth]

Seelia didn't have a chance to see what happened as she had concerns of her own. Two squat looking characters were climbing over the roof tops towards her. One was spinning a long weighted chain over his head the other had a net that was crackling with electricity. It looked as if they intended to take her alive. Seelia ran to meet them.

She vaulted a narrow divide and as she landed thumped her staff into the side of a swirling metal vent. Seelia ripped it free and threw it up into the air. With perfect timing she swung the metal staff and hit the vent as it fell. It span out across the rooftops and smacked the chain wielding attacker in the face. Spinning the staff over in her fingers she launched it like a spear. The tapered end thunked into the chest of the net carrier. He fell backwards and the electrified mesh fell over him. He spasmed as the voltage burned criss-cross patterns through his tunic.

Seelia leapt onto the chest of the other. He spat out a tooth. Seelia grabbed the chain and wrapped it around his neck. She drew back trying to avoid his groping arms. His grubby fingers scratched at her forearms but she quickly tightened the linked noose and his arms fell limply to his side.

A message alert pinged on her visor. It was from Srisk.

The Ecclesiarch charged headlong towards the end of the street firing plasma rounds into the corner of the building. As the wall disintegrated he blasted one of the cowering warriors from his feet but before he could continue his onslaught the ground opened up and he tumbled into a silver walled pit. The roof to the hole slid back across, sealing Srisk inside. The Ecclesiarch vented his Achilles pistons and launched himself upwards. He dented the metal lid but nothing more. He froze as he heard motors wind up. The left and right walls suddenly jolted and started to move inwards.

He sent a message to Seelia.

[Need some help]

As the walls closed in Srisk tried to brace them. The crushing power of the rams easily overwhelmed the Ecclesiarch's suit. Unexpectedly the walls stopped. A panel in front of Srisk slid open to reveal a monitor. He watched as it blinked to life and the City of the Lost logo tumbled across the screen. It was replaced by a graphic of a dial. One side was labelled 'Yes' and the other 'No'. A question tapped across the display.

[Do you want Marin to live? Vote now!]

It took Srisk a second to relate to the fact that he was Marin. He watched as the digital needle swung from one side to the other all for dramatic effect. He was genuinely surprised when finally the needle landed on the 'Yes' vote. The screen faded and another message appeared.

[The public have voted in your favour. Enjoy your stay in the City of the Lost.]

The dented roof slid back and Seelia's confused face peered over the edge. She held a smoking bolt rifle in her hand. She linked with Srisk's mind.

<Hurry and get up here. I think we've found our new crew member.>

The Ecclesiarch landed in the dusty street with a whump. The pair looked down the road where a crowd of would be assailants were failing to stop the rampaging beast within their midst. Whole, and parts of bodies flew into the air as Ortig ripped them to pieces.

Srisk looked down at Seelia, who stood open mouthed.

"You know what to do."

She nodded.

Srisk strode towards the massacre. As the Ecclesiarch approached he casually picked off the soldiers who had decided to leave the fray. By the time he had reached Ortig the street had been turned into a bloody charnel-house. They locked eyes. Srisk could see the fury burning behind Ortig's orange orbs. The stone skinned behemoth moved with incredible speed and although Srisk blocked the first blow the second knocked him backwards. His legs flew out underneath him and he face planted into the dust. Srisk recovered quickly and shaking the sand from his hood readied himself. Ortig clamped his massive hands around the Ecclesiarch's neck. The pressure was greater than that of the trap walls he had just escaped from. In a second his suit would rupture and the mighty Calabrian would pop his head from his shoulders.

Srisk took a deep breath as he heard his choke brace snap. Just then Seelia appeared behind the stone leviathan and snapped the metal collar around his neck. The monstrous warrior roared and flung his arm backwards knocking Seelia to the floor, but it was too late. Srisk had already synched with the device and powered it up. Ortig released his grip and stood dazed as if he had just woken up.

"My name is Srisk. That is my associate Seelia. We would like you to come with us." Srisk suggested.

"Okay" said Ortig.

Srisk connected with his telepathic colleague.

<I told you it would be easy.>

<We still have another three days in this hell hole.>

<I never intended to stay for the entire duration.>

Srisk returned his focus to the swaying creature in front of him.

"I have someone who can help us. Follow me."

"Okay" said Ortig.

They moved down the street until they reached South and second. Srisk was about to knock on the first door when another further down the side street opened and its occupant beckoned them forward. Srisk struggled to squeeze through the narrow doorway. The door jambs cracked and splintered as Ortig ducked into the building. The Volcanian that greeted them smiled revealing several missing teeth.

"I am Moreallis. You are the Ecclesiarch?"

"I am" replied Srisk.

"I have what you need. It is in the basement. We have tunnelled as deep as we are able."

"Show me" demanded Srisk.

The group filed down stone steps into the basement of the building. There were piles of dirt stacked in boxes all around the room. In the floor ahead was a large hole. Srisk looked over the edge and saw the metal plate of the city platform. The Volcanian indicated towards a large shiny black crate. Srisk opened the container and removed four large arcs. He leapt into the hole and assembled the four pieces to form a perfect circle. He clambered back out and connected to the equipment.

Moreallis tapped him on the forearm.

"You are sure we can all leave once you have gone?"

"Give us until morning and then Yes you are free to do what you need" replied Srisk.

The Ecclesiarch activated the ring and bright white light lit up the room. A fizzing noise filled the air as the phosphorous ate its way through the metal floor. Several moments later they heard a loud clank as the circular plug hit the studio floor below.

"Liktus is on his way to meet us." informed Srisk.

Seelia opened a mind-link.

<Please tell me the next one is not a mass murderer?>

Srisk turned to look at the calm and collected Ortig.

"No. He is not. He is much worse."

Sons of Terminus

If there was one star system that embodied the Federation's ideal then it would be that of Tectus-Statera and in particular the five planets that orbited the red dwarf of Theocentricus. They had been thrust into galactic machinations in the early years of the Moretti invasion. They had embraced the war with an unhealthy zeal.

Their well trained and extremely disciplined soldiers formed the front lines of the Federation's defence. They were born for battle. Encased from head to toe in Crusader power armour they became the iconic symbols of defiance for the multi-racial population of FOUR. More gallantry crosses had been awarded to the worlds of Theocentricus than the rest of the star systems combined.

In the recent years of fragile peace they had focused on the expansion of their empire. The Shakari galaxy was vast. Though it had been thousands of years since the Prime worlds had advanced into deep space, most of it still remained unexplored. Outside of the huge sectors that had already been affirmed, lay a plethora of planets just waiting for the flag of Theocentricus to claim them.

The five worlds consisted of: Genus Novus, Kas, Gravitas, Davum and Genus Centricus. The latter considering itself to be the centre of all things, at least from a philosophical point of view. The majority of Theocentricus' forces were stationed along the Defensive Necklace in a constant, and some would say, hopeful vigil. Other battle-groups were used by the Federation to quell uprisings or subdue those that were reluctant to sign the edicts of FOUR. The remaining armies ventured into deep space looking for conquest or securing what they already considered part of their empire.

The regimented mass of force was broken down into distinct fighting units. The smallest entity was known as a Lupiti or Pack. It consisted of nine Optio-Immunis soldiers or Lupitus, and was lead by a Principal. Ten Lupiti was called a Hastati and was governed by a Centurio. Ten Hastati made a Legati and the senior rank of a Legatus ruled over the total thousand person unit. Each Legati was fiercely independent and flew their colours with blusterous pride.

It was a ten man Pack from the Sons of Terminus Order that braced against their harnesses as the Lammergeyer assault craft was buffeted by the cosmic winds. It wasn't the turbulence or the chilling vacuum of space that caused the uncomfortable icy atmosphere within the hold. The reason for the unvoiced malcontent stood towards the prow. He stroked his tattooed head with his power gauntlet. Centurio Agorius Millus.

It wasn't the irregular line of command that saw a Centurio leading a Pack instead of their trusted Principal that caused the restlessness within the squad. It was the rumour that fluttered behind the stern looking Agorius like an unwanted battle pennant. For a civilisation based on honour and order, trust was a fundamental attribute for any in a position of authority. To lose it, or even have it tainted would seriously affect the ability to command. It didn't matter if they were rumours, or that they were rumours based on lies.

Centurio Agorius had fallen foul of political wrangling in a power struggle between a rising Legatus and a failing Senatus. Agorius had followed his orders to the letter. He had identified the possible failings in a proposed stratagem but had been ignored. When the losses came flooding in, as Agorius had predicted, he became the scapegoat. Before he could lodge a formal complaint he had found himself in command of a Pack on a pointless mission far from Theocentricus.

He had been charged with responding to a distress beacon on a rogue planet. The galaxy was full of such worlds, celestial bodies that had no parent star. Instead they wandered the darkness of space on a voyage of change which would ultimately end in oblivion. These rogue planets had provided suitable targets for the expansion of the Theocentricus Empire. They were often heavy with valuable minerals or gas, unpopulated and depending on their trajectory could offer strategic platforms, if not immediately then in their unpredictable future.

The wide winged Lammergeyer was headed to one such planet. It was referenced as TRP86. According to the history log it had supported a exploratory colony of three thousand souls. These were common research groups that consisted of scientists, construction workers, and usually a single Optio-Immunis that was looking for promotion. The harsh and often erratic journey of these rogue planets was a challenge of survival. Any soldier proving his metal in this inhospitable environment would be looked on favourably for advancement. Whoever had been stationed on TRP86 had failed. The distress beacon was only to be activated in the case of an excision event.

The Recit crackled breaking the unspoken tension within the hold.

"One quarter hora until descent."

Agorius looked up to the faceted speaker ball. He opened a comms channel with the pilot.

"What are the readings?" he asked.

"Zero on all fronts Centurio."

Agorius pondered the response. That simple sentence meant no electrical outputs, no atmosphere and no life-forms detected.

"At least without an atmosphere the journey down to the surface will be smoother."

Agorius had no idea why he had just said that. They all knew what 'Zero on all fronts' meant.

The majority of these rogue planets would have long since had any atmosphere scrubbed clean during its hazardous lifespan. Most outposts that clung to these dead worlds constructed bio-domes. Some were small and capable of supporting food farms, others were enormous and enclosed entire colonies. For the occasional, unique world, the power of the planet core would be harnessed and gargantuan belchers would discharge a complex combination of chemicals in order to create a breathable atmosphere and a shield against cosmic radiation. The process could take hundreds of years. TRP86 had nothing, at least nothing that was working.

Agorius stared for a moment at his armoured hand. He once again rubbed it over his bald tattooed skull. It was becoming a habit. He looked at the waiting soldiers. Whatever their opinions of him, they were hardened Lupiti and they waited for his orders.

"Helmets on. Weapon check" Instructed Agorius. He squelched his Recit and addressed the pilot. "Kranos, take us down slowly. Circle pass. To the South of the hab-blocks. Full scan."

"Understood Centurio. Commencing run."

Agorius watched as one by one his Pack covered their painted grey heads with their Valkyrie pattern helms. Bright blue visor slits illuminated and a cacophony of metallic clicks echoed through the hold as each soldier checked their weapon. The Centurio was the last to slide the weighty headgear over his scalp. It clicked into place and hissed as the seal was made. Agorius could see his reflection on the inside of the narrow glass eye-slit.

He had a protruding ridge above his sunken yellow eyes, two small nose slits sat above his thin lipped mouth and a series of metal studs decorated his square jaw line. A tattooed 'Tauri' stretched down over his forehead and the spiral mark of 'The Sons of Terminus' sat beneath his left eye socket. Agorius tried to blink the reflected vision away.

The star-ship banked steeply as it made a first pass.

Kranos made his report.

"Still reading zero on all scans. Temperature reading minus thirty-four. No obvious damage to the habs or the dome. Only power source active is the beacon. The flag is still flying over the temple. Looks like

'White Claws'." There were several derisive grunts from the pack. "What next Centurio?" asked Kranos.

"Put us down near the temple datum. Seal the ship once we have left. Full defensive mode, and Kranos, release my Stallium."

"Understood. Kranos out."

The booster jets roared and the Lammergeyer reared upwards. Agorius heard the hiss as the detachable cargo pod clamps let go. Darkness swamped the Pack and a single red light flashed indicating that the rear ramp was being dropped. The ship bucked as fierce winds outside whipped over its shell. With the ramp only narrowly open the external blizzard entered the hold. The icy tendrils of the dead world reached in to find the heat sources that had dared to violate it.

One by one the Lupiti leapt into the white out. Agorius was the last to leave.

"May the 'Tauri' grant us strength and favour" he muttered to himself.

The Centurio thumped into the snow. The weight of his articulated armour caused him to sink up to his waist before his metal boots hit the rocky surface. He swivelled to see the Lammergeyer rise into the air and the orange glow of its burners lit the snow-filled sky. The ship banked and then its jets flared again as it landed a short distance away. The well trained Pack had already formed an attack triangle and were weapons ready.

"Sound off" ordered Agorius.

"Alaris"

"Bellator"

"Pelekus"

"Caligatus"

"Gallicus"

"Venator"

"Questar"

"Gregarious. Pack ready Centurio."

Agorius didn't know these soldiers but he smiled at their precision and expertise.

He turned to the cargo pod and tapped the green flashing 'activate' button. The sides suddenly thumped into the snow and the huge automaton inside cantered out. The Stallium was a legacy piece of equipment. They were rarely used in modern warfare but Agorius loved tradition. The four legged machine was a crude replica of the ancient animals that had once carried the Theocentrican ancestors into battle. They had long since become extinct. The metal chargers had replaced them.

The Stallium lowered its head as Agorius approached. It had complex artificial intelligence and had been imbued with the digital spirit of its primogenitor in both response and temperance. The igneous valves vented hot steam from its circular nostrils, immediately melting patches of snow. Agorius grabbed the pommel and in one swift movement vaulted onto the machine's back. His armour clicked into the cantle and his suit connected with the Stallium's enhanced sensor array. Agorius leant forward and idly patted the side of the automaton's head.

"Pack advance. Wide spread on my point" Agorius voiced into his helm's Recit.

The metal charger ploughed easily through the soft covering of snow and the squad fanned out into a long line either side of their mounted leader. Agorius scrolled through his connections checking the vital signs of each soldier. The bitter wind scoured their battle-suits and the heavy snowfall made visibility less than ten cliks. He would be their eyes and ears.

Agorius continued to cycle through his steed's sensors looking for any anomaly. The planet was truly dead. Only the pulsating location of the distress beacon featured on his head-up display.

They made their way slowly towards the temple. It would be the remit of the assigned Optio-Immunis to organise construction of a stronghold which he would use to communicate with his Order. It would act as a home, office, fortress and if needed, a prison. They were known as temples. Most followed a pyramidal construction, and this one was no exception. Strangely it had been built some distance from the hab-blocks.

As they approached the snow shrouded building they could see the main door was open and snow had piled up on the approach ramp. An orange light alerted Agorius to a warning code for one of his Pack. He tabbed the display to Gallicus. His thermocouple was indicating a dropping temperature. In the extreme cold it looked as if the thermic-circulation of his suit was failing.

"Gallicus. Double time. Secure the ramp" ordered Agorius.

Appreciating the warmth the exercise would generate the soldier leapt through the snow and climbed towards the entrance to the temple. He held his Strike-rifle high to his shoulder and swept from left to right. There were clear signs of a fire-fight. Plasma burns scored the door frame, and several black shadows stained the chequer-plate floor. Gallicus carefully moved inside the temple.

His sensors scanned the snow covered interior. All of the equipment was dead. The only sign of life was the central beacon. It pulsed with red light powered by its own battery source. Something was very wrong with this situation. Gallicus started as his Recit crackled.

"Report."

"Signs of a fight all over the place. Plasma weaponry by the looks of it. Can't tell if its Legati or something else. Whatever happened here, someone, or something put up quite a defence. There are black marks on the floors and walls. Do you want me to sample them?"

"You need to get that unit up and running first. Will it restart?"

Gallicus walked to the command console and flicked several switches. He followed the armoured cabling to a box high up on the wall. He pulled down on a lever and the cover opened. A small prong extended from his gauntlet and Gallicus touched it to the breakers.

"There's no power. I guess it was fed from the main hab. We'll need to find the reactor."

Gallicus turned quickly as he picked up movement from the corner of his visor. He levelled his gun and his finger tensed on the trigger. His eyes and his scans returned nothing. Gallicus lowered the weapon. He opened a channel on his Recit.

"Orders?"

"How long do you have before your suit is compromised?" asked Agorius.

"One ten hora" lied Gallicus.

"Return to the Lammergeyer. Get it fixed. A frozen soldier is no good to me."

Gallicus thought of arguing but he knew the Centurio was right. In these temperatures without a heat flow he would be dead within an hora. He slapped the gauntlets of his comrades as he walked down the ramp and then quickly disappeared into the whiteness.

"Who is the Pack Tech-Elder?" asked Agorius.

Questar held his arm aloft as he walked past the motionless steed and up the ramp.

"See if you can retrieve any data. We need to know what happened here. Alaris, Bellator defensive posts at the door. The rest of you pair up. Fifteen clik patrol from my mark. Anything, and I mean anything, call it in."

"As you command" came the unified response.

Agorius accessed his Stallium's controls. This was unusual. The scans were blank. Even the vast arrays aboard the Lammergeyer had returned zero. Where had the three thousand settlers gone? If there had been a fight then where were the bodies? The bio-reads would have picked up any signs of life, no matter how faint. Maybe they had left? After all TRP86 held no great significance. It was probably why he had been sent here.

Gunfire sounded in his ear.

Agorius swivelled and leapt from the saddle. His armoured boots clanked as he ran up the ramp with his bolt pistol drawn. Gun flashes illuminated the dark interior and he could hear the spent shells skittling across the consoles. His visor adjusted for the low light as he entered and he could see Questar, Alaris and Bellator strafing rounds high up on the angular ceiling. He looked up but couldn't see any signs of an enemy.

"Cease fire" he bellowed.

The barked order broke the Pack's focus and they released their fingers from their triggers.

"There was something there" insisted Questar.

Agorius switched on the spotlight mounted to the side of his helm. Just like on the ramp and the floor of the temple there was a black stain in amongst the hundreds of bullet holes and hanging electrical debris. Agorius opened a Recit channel.

"Return to the temple immediately."

Both pairs on patrol acknowledged his order.

"Can you power one of these monitors from your suit? We need to replay your video feed."

Questar nodded and set to work ripping cables from the instrument panel and plugging them into his suit. By the time he was ready the other four members of the Lupiti had returned. They all stared intently at the static plagued picture as the Tech-Elder replayed his helm's video recording.

"There. Freeze that" ordered Agorius.

"What is it?" asked Bellator.

"I would guess that it is the reason the distress beacon was initiated. It is alien life of some form but nothing I have ever seen before."

"Why is it not showing on our scans?" asked Bellator.

"I do not know" admitted Agorius. "Zoom in."

The four limbed creature was almost skeletal. Long, thin black arms and legs both ending in a series of knife-life claws. An articulated tail, that looked like a series of vertebrae also ended in a curved blade. Its narrow head had black needle like spines running in a line from its snout back over its jet black scalp. The most striking feature was its mouth. It ran almost the full length of its skull and was packed full of glistening translucent teeth. The creature's skin looked as if it was highly polished. Its black gloss carapace reflected its surroundings like a mirror.

Agorius moved to a patch of the black discolouring on the floor plates. He moved the snow away with his foot and then scraped the dark substance with his finger.

"Who has the spectrometer?" he asked.

Venator pushed past his comrades and held out the equipment. Agorius placed his dust covered finger onto the scan plate. The machine bleeped intermittently and then a constant tone.

"What does it say?" asked Agorius.

"Silica of some type. That would explain why our sensors aren't picking anything up. They are calibrated for carbon and boron life forms. I have never heard of a complex silicon based creature."

"Who knows where this planet has travelled. There are still many mysteries in this galaxy. Can you re-calibrate the array on the Lammergeyer?"

"Yes Centurio" nodded Questar.

"Then let's move. We have no idea what we are up against. Double time back to the ship."

Agorius had not even made it back to his waiting Stallium when the sky erupted with light. The explosion shook the ground and the subsequent shock wave knocked the entire pack from their feet. Flame, gas and molten plasma vented in a rainbow of colours as the Lammergeyer's power plant fractured and the Pack's transport disintegrated in a deafening detonation. Parts of the star ship were thrown high into the air and the surrounding snowscape was evaporated. Agorius's visor display was a series of flashing red warnings as the heat wave washed over him. He ignored his suit's advisories and clambered to his feet. In the distance he could see further explosions as the Lammergeyer's gun magazines ruptured. Set against the grey snowy backdrop he could see hundreds of skittering shapes running from the chaotic outbursts.

"Kranos. Gallicus. Do you copy?"

There was only static.

"Damn it." cursed Agorius. He jumped up onto the Stallium. Part of him desired to charge headlong towards the hideous horde of creatures, but he knew that was not an option. Not yet at least.

"Get to your feet" he ordered. "We'll follow the conduit back towards the hab. We have to get a message out. Caligatus put a charge on that beacon. I want it destroyed."

"It is our only locator Centurio" argued Questar. "If it is destroyed and we cannot find a comms link then the Order will have no way of finding this planet."

"That is correct. Whatever these things are, they are intelligent. The beacon was designed to bring us here. We cannot let another Pack walk into the same trap. Now set that charge and let's move."

Without further dissent, the explosives were planted and the remaining Lupiti chased their way along the snow covered mound which linked the temple to the hab-blocks.

Agorius galloped ahead, his mechanical charger flinging snow into the sky behind it. He had his sights set on the faded outline of the buildings ahead and didn't notice movement to his right until it was too late. The creature leapt from the snow its savage rows of teeth gaping open. Agorius had not noticed it as it had changed its colour. The shiny black skin they had witnessed back at the temple was now white. He reached up and grabbed the animal around the throat. It didn't have any eyes but it seemed to know exactly where to strike. Its jaws gnashed at his helm and its long blade-like talons of its forearms sliced at his armour, whilst its rear legs clawed at his steed. Agorius swiftly drew his bolt pistol and rammed it into the creature's mouth shattering its icicle teeth. He pulled the trigger and the silicon entity evaporated in a white mist, its alien substance mixing invisibly with the falling snow.

He was aware of movement all around. He activated the Stallium's defensive arsenal as he halted his mount. The mechanical steed reared into the air before thumping its forelegs into the white powder. A furious salvo erupted from its haunches vaporising the alien host in front of them. Agorius slid from his saddle and unhitched the Graphene baton that was locked to his thigh. At that moment the temple explosive detonated and a fiery plume rose behind the fleeing Pack.

The rest of the Lupiti were running and firing as the white bladed creatures came invisibly out of the snowstorm. Agorius stood with his back to his Stallium and systematically picked off those that made it close to his squad. He toggled the power switch on the baton and the light-hammer buzzed with life. A glowing block of light appeared. It spat white sparks as it hummed its power tune.

"On my mark. Regroup" ordered the Centurio.

Each Pack member homed in on their leader and as each arrived they set up a defensive firing pattern around the Stallium that had already inflicted heavy losses. Bolt fire mixed with fizzing blue plasma creating a wall of death.

"Alaris. Move it."

Agorius could see his heat signature on his visor overlay. He was struggling, seemingly firing erratically in every direction.

"Check your targets!" bellowed Agorius.

"I am. They're everywhere" the soldier yelled in reply.

Agorius's bolt pistol blasted the clawing white figures until the magazine emptied. He clamped the weapon back to his hip and hefted the light hammer with both hands. It purred in his gauntlets as he ran towards the straggling soldier. Alaris was being overwhelmed. Multiple claw strikes had found the weaknesses in his armour and the creature's long blades now dug into his flesh through the minute gaps. Undeterred, Alaris activated his energy claws. Two serrated blades emerged from the back of each vambrace and blue light danced along the edges. The stubborn soldier tore into the silicon foe with a matched venom. He suffered several strikes to his right leg. He could feel the warm blood trickle down inside his suit and finally his joint gave out and he fell to one knee. One creature leapt directly at his face. Its needle like teeth scraped the paint and scored his visor before his power claw ripped its chest in half. The alien life form disintegrated only to be replaced by another. Alaris growled as he sought to fend off the next attacker.

Bright white light almost blinded him. He heard the hum and saw the glowing head of Agorius's hammer smash into the creature's body. The injured soldier breathed a brief sigh of relief as he watched the Centurio spin like a deadly gyroscope into the alien throng.

Alaris held out his hand towards his commander. Agorius reached for him and grabbed his armoured gauntlet. As the Centurio attempted to pull him up a shiny white entity landed on the back of Alaris. It stabbed down frenziedly at the outstretched arm, and in a scream of anguish the severed arm of the stricken Optio-Immunis came away in Agorius's hand.

The Centurio looked on in horror as the creatures swarmed over the bleeding body of Alaris. Their long bladed claws opened his armour like a can of convenience food, and the white heads ripped into his flesh devouring the soldier even as he screamed his last breath. Within moments they had stripped his bones clean.

Cursing into his re-breather Agorius staggered backwards. The reason for these creature's fury was now obvious. They were starving.

As he returned to the remaining Pack he saw patches of red staining the white canvas. They were all running low on ammunition, even his Stallium would eventually run dry. They would have their melee weapons but as he had witnessed they would be quickly overrun. They had to make it to the hab-block. Agorius could see the central spire through the flurry of snow. The bio-dome would normally have shimmered around it. Even without atmosphere it was their only chance. Out in the open they would die.

He accessed his Stallium's on board navigation and directed the four-legged automaton towards the buildings ahead. He opened a Recit channel to the remaining Pack.

"Follow my steed. Bellator, Caligatus forward fire, the rest of you, rearguard action with me."

The research colony was barely five hundred cliks away. It may as well have been a light year.

One by one, the weapons emptied and the fighting got personal. Power fists and energy hammers crackled into life as the desperate squad tried to keep the never ending alien horde at bay. In synchronised perfection the remaining seven warriors parried and struck like a single minded organism. They would not submit. They had skill. They had belief. That morale took a blow when the Stallium discharged its final round and turned from a defensive bastion into a mechanical statue.

It was Questar who broke the focused concentration of battle.

"Centurio. You must get to the hab. We will provide what distraction we can."

"I'm not leaving" demanded Agorius.

"One of us must get a message back to the Order. Go, before it's too late."

Agorius ran through the bloody slush and vaulted onto the back of the Stallium.

"Sons of Terminus I salute you" he said as the rear legs of the massive machine powered them forwards. He didn't want to leave. He would be the Centurio that had lost yet more good soldiers, the leader that had deserted his Pack in their moment of need. His gut twisted as he knew this was the right course of action. He would die on this miserable rock, but first he would get a message out. Duty demanded it. He owed that to his adopted Pack.

As the outer silhouette of the steel buildings showed through the blizzard he heard the roar of jets above. He looked to the sky trying to determine, who or what had arrived. He could make out the orange pulse of burners but the white flurry of snowflakes obscured his view. The distraction cost him dearly as the Stallium caught its foreleg on a snow covered rock and buckled into the powder. Agorius was sent flying from his saddle. He rolled on his shoulder and stood with his light hammer ready. The clashing of teeth and claws surrounded him. All discipline suddenly slipped away. The mission fell from his mind like an unwanted memory and was replaced by anger. His lip curled and he howled a battle cry at his silicon enemy.

Warning icons flashed on the Centurio's visor as his suit was compromised. He couldn't feel the cold seep in through the cracks or the razor sharp blades that sought to open him up. His light hammer continued to rise and fall but all he could see were the nine blinking symbols of the rest of his Lupiti. Each one flat-lined.

Agorius grimaced as a long talon buried deep into his shoulder. He twisted, breaking the creature's finger and then smashed the glowing hammer into the beast's head. It evaporated and Agorius stumbled forward. He heard the teeth gnash above him but it was followed by the loud crack of gunfire. He righted himself to see three figures running through the frozen storm. They fired as they moved. They were not from Theocentricus.

A tall hooded figure skidded towards him. He thumped a staff into the ground as his two companions joined him. The metal pole telescoped upwards and a personal force shield domed over their heads. The white horde clattered against the energy field.

The hooded warrior held out his hand in a sign of friendship. The Centurio refused to take it.

"Who are you?" asked Agorius.

"I am Srisk. We do not have much time. This shield won't last long."

"I am not going anywhere" said Agorius. "My Pack lies dead. I cannot leave. I will die here with them. I cannot face the shame."

"Your comrades must be avenged. Your path does not end here Centurio Agorius Millus. You are being called to serve something greater. I will explain all. After that, if you feel you would still like to remain, then I will happily leave you here."

"The shield is failing!" called his slender compatriot.

"Ortig, you'll need to buy us some time" said Srisk.

The huge stone-like warrior looked confused.

"What you want me to do?" it asked.

"Those things" The hooded figure pointed to the creatures that swarmed around the protective hemisphere. "Kill them."

The giant creature looked worried.

"They will hurt me" it pleaded.

"You'll be fine" assured Srisk. "Liktus. On our position now. Drop the lines."

Agorius looked up as three steel cables swung through the air. The thin female was the first to connect just as the shield started to fade. The hooded warrior grabbed the other two connectors and clamped one onto his suit before handing the other to Agorius.

"What about him?" Agorius nodded to the startled Ortig, who now looked genuinely frightened.

"There are only three hoists. Take it now, and don't worry about him."

Agorius took the karabiner and snapped it onto his shoulder hook. As soon as it clicked into place he was lifted from his feet. The shield collapsed and the white alien mass poured in. They bristled around Ortig who feebly tried to bat them away.

"Srisk!" he called out. "Help me!"

Agorius watched as the cloaked newcomer tapped his control pad. He looked directly at the Centurio and then pointed below.

"Watch" he said calmly.

Agorius could no longer see the other warrior. He was covered in a swarming throng of bladed limbs. Suddenly they erupted upwards in a scrambling silicon fountain. The giant warrior thumped his chest and roared against the blizzard. As Agorius was pulled higher he lost sight of the rampaging Ortig as he shredded the alien creatures.

*

"My name is Ecclesiarch Srisk. This is Seelia and our friend down there is Ortig. We'll pick him up once he has had enough exercise. It's good for him to blow off some steam."

"How do you know my name?" asked Agorius.

"Have you heard of the Lords of the Balance?" asked Srisk.

"They are not real" answered Agorius.

"They are very real my friend and they sent me to find you. Just in time by the look of things."

Agorius snorted.

"What is it you want?"

"I do not want anything from you" replied Srisk. "My masters however, require your service. The fragile peace that exists in this galaxy is no mere coincidence. You have fought for Theocentricus since you were old enough to wield a blaster. You are now being asked to do that for those who keep the balance, for those who maintain the peace. We are the hands that pull the strings."

"What of my Order?"

"As far as your Order is concerned you were lost on this world along with your brave brothers. Which of course, as I promised, is still an option if you wish to stay." suggested Srisk calmly.

The indicators on Agorius's visor display flashed green and he touched a finger to the retaining clips. The air hissed as the helm popped free. He ran his gauntleted hand over his tattooed scalp.

"I would warn you that as a Centurio of Theocentricus I may find it difficult taking orders from one who is not indoctrinated in the ways of our Order."

The Ecclesiarch stood and adjusted his cloak.

"Change is essential to growth my friend. What you were is no longer important, it is what you will become that will shape your life now." Srisk held out his hand. "Welcome Agorius, Warrior of the Balance."

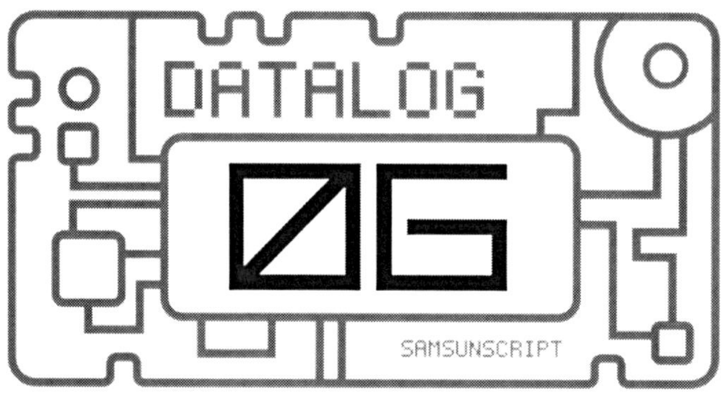

Dawn of Light

Two years later.

*

"Can't this barge go any faster?" demanded Agorius.

"It's a cargo freighter, it's not designed for speed" answered the small red creature.

"We'll be there soon enough" added Srisk.

"The plan is thin Ecclesiarch. I will not let the Baron slip from my gauntlet for a third time. The sooner we dock with his cruiser and unload this damned payload, the safer I will feel."

"I want him as much as you do, but anything suspicious or out of schedule could betray us. You know how cautious he is. If I am being honest I am amazed we have made it this far."

A red light started to blink on the helm controls, shortly followed by a rasping klaxon. Liktus scrambled across the vast expanse of buttons and flicked a switch to acknowledge the warning. He turned to the Ecclesiarch.

"It's the upper hold, the halon has been triggered. Isn't Seelia down there?"

Srisk tapped out a message.

[What's happening?]

[Hold on...] came the reply.

[Who loaded this stuff? These containers are antiques, the cryo-chambers are all struggling to keep the gas at temperature. I have been re-routing the power linkages but the ship's sensors must have picked up a trace. You know what will happen if this stuff mixes with a carrier don't you?]

[We are all aware of its volatility. Is it secure?]

[For now. Two hours max. Then it needs to be moved into a proper refrigeration unit or alternatively we need to be far away from it.]

"What's going on?" asked Agorius.

Srisk ignored the question and looked at Liktus.

"Can't this bucket move any faster?".

*

Once the Ecclesiarch had sent word to the Noxvata that he had acquired his final team member the orders of their mission had filtered through almost instantly. There was an urgency he had not detected before. They had been instructed to capture and return the errant son of Keterus-Alpha, Baron Valah, to the Ninth Cloud.

The twin Prime worlds of Keterus-Alpha and Keterus-Beta were located in the same star system as Theocentricus. Whereas the latter provided the brawn for the Federation, the ancient households of Keterus had always been on the cusp of technological discovery. Their inventions and designs had made the galaxy a smaller and safer place to live.

An edict had been issued by the ruling Household of Keterus-Alpha against the Baron for high treason. He was a major prize. He had every Ghost, Ghoul and Wraith on his trail. It was testament to Valah's tenacity that he had managed to avoid capture. Srisk had realised that was the reason his sister, the Baroness Rainah, had approached the Lords of the Balance. She had hoped their clandestine soldiers would affect a quicker solution. How disappointed must she be? Srisk and his team had come close on several occasions but Valah always seemed to be one step ahead. Agorius had long since forgotten the original mission, it was now almost a personal vendetta. The regimented ways of the Legati would stay with him forever.

All direct incursions or attempted abductions had failed. Srisk rethought his strategy.

The Baron had commandeered one of the Cursus fleet's colossal battle cruisers. The 'Dawn of Light' was the very latest edition to the Federation's navy. Over two kilometres in length it was equipped with enough firepower to cleanse an entire world, and housed a fleet of more than six hundred strike fighters and was home to more than a quarter of a million souls. So it was a surprise to all the authorities and Srisk's team when the ship simply vanished. It's whereabouts had been a mystery ever since.

The Ecclesiarch's plan had been one of simplicity. They had little chance of finding the Baron if he did not want to be found, so they would engineer a situation whereby the Baron would find them.

Most ships ran on hydrogen fusion which was clean and efficient and relatively safe. The newest generation of vessels had opted to use the atomic nuclei of a less than stable gas, Phenophyre. It was more commonly known as 'dancing gas' due to the effects it had on most races' physiology - it destroyed cell structure, causing the body to fit and spasm as if performing some contemporary dance pattern. Despite its hazardous nature the output was vastly superior and worth the compromise.

The new fuel had borne an exploratory industry and a race of galactic corporations to exploit it. Without it, the mighty 'Dawn of Light' would be just another stationary celestial object. Baron Valah could not risk any controlled outlet, all of them were closely monitored by the Agency. He had to venture into the sordid belly of the Netherverse and deal with the pirates and other nefarious types that traded without the rules or restrictions of the overbearing Federation.

Srisk had located one such band of criminals that had recently entered into the theft and resale of Phenophyre. The 'Church of the Raven' as they were collectively known had acquired a large shipment of the dangerous gas and had brokered a deal with a character they referred to as the White Baron. The murderous gang were more than a little surprised when their stolen cargo was again the subject of a counter-heist.

FOUR - Warriors of the Balance -Samsun Lobe

*

Liktus double checked the navigation coordinates.

"Check it again" demanded Agorius.

Srisk stepped in.

"If he says we are in the right place, then we are."

"Then where is the Baron? I'm sure that not even he can hide a Sovereign battle cruiser in plain sight" complained Agorius. The ex-Centurio could not hide his frustration. He turned to Ortig who sat towards the rear of the bridge. The solitary Calabrian had recently taken to knitting. The large metal needles clanked together in a metallic rhythm.

"Do you have to do that now?" asked Agorius.

"It's soothing" replied Ortig.

Agorius shook his head and looked into the hood of Srisk.

"Do you think Valah knows something?" he asked.

"Maybe" admitted the Ecclesiarch. "But even if he does, my guess is he would risk it for the chance to get his hands on this cargo."

"Then where is he?"

Agorius walked to the command console.

"Where is that tracking beacon control? We should turn it off. If the Baron is not here, then I seriously doubt we want to be sat waiting when the Church of the Raven catch up with us."

The conversation was abruptly interrupted as numerous alarms and warning lights filled the bridge.

"What is it?" asked Srisk.

"The proximity alarm" replied Liktus.

As they looked out from the narrow cockpit windows the 'Dawn of Light' unveiled alongside them. A wall of flickering shields, towering armaments filled every viewport as the colossal battle cruiser shed its cloak of stealth. It was enormous, overpoweringly massive. Huge hangar gates started to open like the mouth of some ancient mechanical leviathan. It growled with menace.

"How is it possible to hide a ship of that size?" asked Agorius. "It didn't even appear on our scanners."

The Ecclesiarch didn't have a chance to reply. The Recit bleeped. Liktus opened a channel.

"This is the Dawn of Light. Do you have the cargo?"

"Yes" replied Srisk. "Do you have the money?"

"You will get what you were promised" came the curt reply.

"Fine. What would like us to do?"

"Nothing. You are in our hands now."

The freighter rocked as a tether line clattered against the hull and the magnetic field of the hangar bay reached out to grab the ship.

"Power down." commanded Srisk. "Cut all engines. Liktus get to the Apocris. Prep for launch, we'll need you to be ready when the time comes."

"Yes master" said the scaled creature.

"Seelia, are you online?"

[Yes] came the text reply.

"I want you with Liktus onboard the Apocris. If he's to stand any chance of making it then he'll need you on the turret gun."

[Understood]

"Can I stay here?" asked Ortig.

"No my friend, we will need your expertise." replied Srisk.

"But I don't have any." The mammoth creature shrugged his stone-like shoulders.

"You'll be fine. Don't worry."

"You always say 'don't worry', that just makes me worry even more."

"Follow Agorius and myself and I promise we will keep you safe."

The unusual threesome disembarked the rusty cargo ship and made their way down the rear loading ramp. There was a uniformed welcoming party. Srisk looked around the cavernous hangar. There were glass-fronted control rooms way up on the walls, each one flanked by blister turrets. The rest of the space was filled with strike fighters and a few much larger bombers. Hundreds of Keterans fussed around them, like insects tending a brooding empress inside a steel and Graphene hive. Most of the hangar residents were engineers or technicians of some description but there were also a notable number of armed troops, similar to the squad that waited to greet them.

Keterans were the definitive type of bipedal genus in the galaxy. They stood upright on two legs, had two arms and hands with long thin fingers. They had pallid skin and were hairless except for a thin covering on their skulls. They had two forward facing eyes, nose and a mouth inset with square, flat teeth. They were much weaker in physical terms than most of the other Prime races but what they lacked in brawn they made up for in intelligence, determination and cunning.

Each of the soldiers wore a lightweight exo-skeleton that more than made up for the wearer's lack of strength. They were each identically armed with a single bolt pistol pinned on their chest plate and an underwhelming assault rifle clutched in their right hands. Thin impact helms covered their heads and a retractable mirrored visor covered their faces. Only the lead soldier revealed his features. He had a glyph painted on his left chest plate that Srisk recognised as the sigil for Sagittarius-a, the super-massive black hole at the centre of the Shakari galaxy. He knew that a cult had adopted the symbol but it was a surprise to see it here.

The lead guard held out his hand.

"That's far enough scavenger" he grunted. "You'll need to leave your weapons with my team. Sorry but those are my orders."

Srisk was carrying his molecular sword and a plasma pistol whilst Agorius had a huge backpack towering over his head and a stubby assault cannon grasped in both hands.

"No I'm sorry" said Srisk. "But there's no chance of that happening."

The Ecclesiarch took a step towards the soldier. Srisk towered above him.

"I'm not intimidated by you marauder types. You are all the same. Credit is all that matters. You needn't worry you'll get your money. Now drop your weapons."

He held his right arm aloft and his squad raised their rifles in unison.

The glow in Srisk's augmented eyes intensified.

"I'm not sure what sort of scavengers you have encountered in the past, but I represent the Church of the Raven. Let me tell you how this is going to play out. My friend and I have an audience with the Baron. This gentle giant..." Srisk pointed towards Ortig. "He will stay here and guard our ship and our precious cargo. Which by the way is wired with explosive. If I suspect any deception I will have no problem in vaporising this hangar and everything in it."

"You're bluffing."

"Am I?" said Srisk. "Well let's find out."

The Ecclesiarch turned and nodded to the confused giant behind him.

"Stay here and make sure no-one enters the ship. I'll send you a message when everything has been settled. Then you can let them in. Do you understand?"

Ortig nodded vaguely.

"Can't I come with you?" he asked meekly.

"It's time to earn your pay" replied Srisk. The tall Ecclesiarch brushed his way past the guard and Agorius followed. "If you have to shoot me captain, then go ahead. You can explain the resulting situation to the Baron." added Srisk.

The squad of Keterans moved aside as the two goliaths strode by.

A perplexed Ortig called out.

"What pay?"

Both Srisk and Agorius ignored their comrade and kept walking towards a security gate marked 'Six B'. As they moved Agorius grabbed two feeds from his tall backpack and plugged them into either side of his gun.

"Think you'll have enough rounds?" asked Srisk.

"We'll find out soon enough" replied Agorius.

"That we will. Time for some chaos." The Ecclesiarch tapped [GO] into his forearm console and then sent the release code to Ortig's collar. Some distance from the docked freighter several explosions rocked the yawning hangar. Fire and smoke plumed upwards and before the fire suppressant could extinguish it, a strike fighter's plasma core vented and ruptured. The resultant blast sent hundreds of bodies flying into the vast chamber.

Ortig had thumped his challenge on his chest before tearing into the armed squad in front of him. Panicked soldiers and engineers now ran in terror as the stone behemoth smashed and pulped his way across the metal mesh floor.

Agorius tapped the switch on his assault cannon and the circular ejector chamber span up to speed. He squeezed the trigger and a barrage of explosive slugs peppered the security gate. Fire blazed from the short muzzle as hundreds of rounds pulverised everything in front of it. Bodies were ripped to pieces by the large calibre rounds and the blast doors connecting the rest of the ship to the hangar bay were obliterated. The metal shrapnel added to the lethal bullet storm.

At that moment the pursuing ships of the real 'Church of the Raven' arrived. One by one the deviant fleet decelerated from hyper-speed homing in on the beacon that Srisk had purposefully left active. Instead of the ageing cargo ship the shocked pirate craft were faced with the monolithic battle cruiser. Both sides seemed to pause for a moment taking in unexpected the situation.

It was the Dawn of Light that fired first. Multiple bursts started to ripple across its flanks as the void started to fill with molten rounds. The salvo was overwhelming and several of the smaller 'Church' craft vanished in the explosive display. Others managed to activate shields, some of the more agile ships dived or rose away from the melee. The buccaneer's flagship was a frigate called 'Vorm's Curse'. It sustained substantial damage to its engines before its shield flickered across the damaged hull. Bank upon bank of automatic missiles swirled back in response. Most exploded in the short space between the two combatant craft as the myriad of rapid firing cannons sought to defend the larger ship. Those projectiles that made it through exploded against the shield like pebbles thrown into a pond. The ripples radiated out in every direction as the undulating armour attempted to absorb the energy. The flurry of missiles had some success as projectiles hit the same spot repeatedly. The flexing shield became weak enough for a Hotspike warhead to penetrate the defence and a molten pulse of death streaked into the depths of the gargantuan cruiser.

The Dawn of Light retaliated as its main armament came on line. Massive twin barrelled cannons erupted lances of light. The burning javelins of plasma scorched through the vacuum of space and burst the feeble shields of Vorm's curse. The Flagship was seared in two. The thousands of gun emplacements on the battle cruiser continued to pour on the devastation as hangar gates opened and a deluge of strike fighters swarmed into the fray.

*

Seelia threw Liktus up into the air. The red creature landed on top of the aircraft. He skitted across the smooth armour and quickly lifted the levers on an access hatch. The pair had chosen the bomber for its close proximity to the outer door. Seelia had taken out most of the crew that were preparing it for flight from a distance. They had also set the charges that were now causing complete mayhem.

She crouched by the front landing leg of the wide winged ship. Unlike the small agile fighters the bombers were fat bodied and had equally inflated wings which housed their density drives and burners. They were designed to carry an enormous payload of ordinance and every feature was engineered for that singular purpose. They had little in the way of personal firepower. A single chin mounted Volt cannon and a rear facing combi-mortar was it.

Seelia breathed out as she pulled the trigger of her sniper rifle. The solitary round took the nearest Keteran through the neck and exited into the face of the soldier standing directly behind him. A spray of crimson blood fountained from the first victim onto the second.

Most of the Keteran force within the hangar had been drawn towards the rampaging Ortig. It was carnage. It had given Seelia and Liktus an opportunity to move unhindered. The access ladder suddenly started to descend from the belly of the bomber. Seelia ran towards it. A bullet ricocheted from one of the rungs and then a second caught her high in the shoulder. She span to see the soldier level his rifle. Seelia fired the sniper rifle without aiming. The high velocity slug punched a hole through the stricken trooper. It clipped his spinal cord, and he fell like a puppet with its strings cut.

Seelia clambered into the ship. The bomb bay was almost empty. A singular forty kiloton shell had been dragged halfway up the ramp. Seelia released the brakes on the cradle and it span back down the slope.

[I'm in. Close the doors] she typed.

Liktus already had the awkward craft airborne by the time she reached the cockpit. She had taken an enviro-suit on her way and stumbled as she tried to get her foot into the trouser leg. She steadied herself against the bulkhead and managed to secure the rest of the suit. She jabbed a medi-pen into her wounded shoulder before she grabbed the spherical glass helmet. She smiled as she clicked the helm into place as it fitted neatly over her headphones. She tapped a message on her console. The task was made more difficult due to the cumbersome gloves.

[Topside now. Get me in position.]

"Yes Miss" replied Liktus.

*

Srisk and Agorius's journey through the ship was one of relative ease. The commotion caused by the arrival of the Church of the Raven had the crew flustered. There were those who remembered protocol and went about their tasks without fuss, but the majority stumbled in a confused daze. Those that were unlucky enough to cross the path of the two intruders were shredded in a hailstorm of bullets.

Srisk had reactivated Ortig's collar in order to communicate with him. He had advised the indestructible warrior to get as far away from the hangar as he could.

"I hope they are all clear" said Srisk.

"I said it was a thin plan" replied Agorius.

Srisk had suspected any communications could have been intercepted by the Baron. To that end they had concocted a plan of misdirection just in case. They had no intention of leaving aboard the Apocris. The reliable fighter had been packed full with high explosive. Srisk had figured that only the cargo would be checked. The crew of the Light of Dawn would have been confident in destroying any foreign ship that tried to get loose inside one of the hangars. He activated the fuse and the massive ship suddenly bucked as the Apocris detonated. White light erupted from the side of the cruiser as the explosion triggered multiple discharges and the unstable cargo of Phenophyre ignited. A wave of violent energy spread like a cancerous star through the ship. A chain reaction of multiple outbursts continued to rock the leviathan.

Srisk touched his gauntlet to the access panel and the door to the bridge slid open.

The crew of the Dawn of Light were all busy on their individual consoles trying to deal with the hundreds of issues that were pouring into their communications. One man stood alone. He was much taller than the rest of the Keterans. He had blonde hair slicked back over his head and had a matching well trimmed beard. He wore a simple tight fitting crimson tunic, and seemed unarmed. He turned as the pair entered. He smiled in an almost sympathetic manner, then fixed them a dark stare.

"Welcome gentlemen. I have to say I am impressed, not surprised but definitely impressed."

"What was it that gave us away?" asked Srisk.

"Price my friend. Price. The thieving Church would never have settled on such a low offer. They would have tried to negotiate at least twice as much. Your eagerness to make the trade made me suspect. Allowing those dirty scavengers to track you though, that was clever. As for the damage you have done to my ship. Fortunately it's not fatal but it is inconvenient to say the least."

"If you knew we were coming then why are you still here?" barked Agorius.

"Your tenacity is inspiring. I decided I would meet you before I kill you. I was interested in seeing those who had managed to get this close to me. I know your masters will send others after you, but that is the lot of one such as myself. Besides I also need the fuel. Tell me Ecclesiarch do you know why you are here?"

"What does that matter?" asked Srisk.

"You follow blindly. I don't believe that." Again the Baron smiled.

"You sister wants you dead" snarled Agorius.

Baron Valah focused on the bristling warrior.

"Theocentrican. You are all the same. You wouldn't be able to survive without orders and regiment. Free thought must scare you." The Baron turned his back for a moment. "So my beloved sister Rainah has turned against me. Well that's no surprise either. She is as power hungry as my father always was."

"It is you that has turned on your people" retorted Agorius.

"You only know what you have been told. You know nothing of the truth. You have been fed lies since you were born into the Legati and now your new masters do the same. The Noxvata are as corrupt as any in this universe." The Baron turned to Srisk. "Tell me Ecclesiarch, you do not accept everything they pronounce? I know you must have your doubts. Why do you still follow their instruction?"

"When all paths are tainted, you follow the least stained."

"You quote The Great Sage as your purpose in life? Surely you have more substance than that."

"I'm sure you believe in what you are doing" answered Srisk. "I have lived through many crusades all of which have had a righteous purpose. They did not change the galaxy. They did not alter our path of existence. So yes, I follow with my eyes closed because open or shut the result is always the same."

"That's a shame" conceded the Baron. "I had hoped to explain what I had unearthed. I thought that you, one of the longest serving Warriors of the Balance would at least hear me out. I do not have a grand vision or even desires of conquest, I simply offer the truth."

"He's stalling" muttered Agorius. "Are we taking him or not?"

Baron Valah moved to touch his fingers to his bare forearm. Agorius did not wait for Srisk's command. He squeezed the trigger and the stubby assault cannon opened up. Screams were drowned out under the 'putt-putt' rhythm of the gun and the chink of shell casings that bounced around the feet of Agorius. Those that did not die instantly in the bullet storm were suddenly sucked from the bridge into the void of space as the onslaught fractured the cockpit glass. Bodies and debris mingled as they tumbled through the shattered window. Both Srisk and Agorius were mag-locked to the floor and had assisted breathing. There was no sign of the Baron.

"We need him alive!" shouted Srisk.

Both warriors stood transfixed as Baron Valah slowly stood upright. He was still only wearing his crimson tunic. He had no breathing apparatus and no obvious way of avoiding the initial pull of the vacuum. As the pressure equalised he started to walk towards them. Agorius fired again. The bullets seemed to bend around the Baron as if an invisible field altered their trajectory, whilst others simply vanished in front of him and reappeared behind at the same velocity. The burning hot muzzle of the assault cannon was silenced as the last round was spent. The whirring buzz of the motor chamber remained as it took Agorius a moment to realise the weapon was no longer firing. He dropped the heavy gun and released the ammunition pack from his back. Agorius drew his light hammer and Srisk twisted the hilt to power up his molecular sword.

"All very crude" said the Baron. "But so predictable. Technology has always been an outward expansion, but I have taken it the other way."

Valah leapt towards Agorius. The crackling hammer head passed harmlessly over him and surprisingly the un-armoured form of the Baron knocked the tank-like warrior from his feet. The Baron formed his fingers into a point and struck downwards. His bare hand punched straight through Agorius's chest armour and into his shoulder. The ex-Centurio roared in pain. Agorius fought against the agony and brought the hammer around. He attempted to smash it into the side of the Baron's head. Valah brought his forearm up to block the strike. For any normal mortal, armoured or not, the power of the light hammer would have shattered the limb and the Baron's skull. Instead his bare arm stopped the weapon dead.

Srisk moved towards the Baron and kicked out with his power suit. Valah back flipped out of reach. His lack of any visible armour gave him complete freedom of movement.

"Impressive" said Srisk. He turned the collar on his sword and small tendrils of lightning dancing along its edge. "But as you say, all so predictable."

Srisk span smoothly and lashed out with the wide bladed weapon. Just as he had hoped the Baron's confidence had blurred his intelligence and instead of easily avoiding the cut he stood proud to let it hit him. He wanted to clearly demonstrate his ascendancy. Srisk had gambled on this moment and the modified sword clashed against the Baron's invisible shield. As the two power sources met a bright white light filled the bridge. Srisk's sword faded as it shorted out.

"Nice try" said Valah.

Srisk looked to the shattered window and watched as the suited figure of Seelia filled the space. She fired her sniper rifle. The Baron didn't have a chance to turn. The Ecclesiarch hoped against all the odds that Valah's shield had been disrupted just long enough. A small black dart thudded into the Baron's neck and he collapsed instantly.

"Good work" said Srisk as Seelia bounced towards them in her enviro-suit. The Ecclesiarch twisted the unconscious Baron's arms behind his back and clamped them together with a set of inhibition cuffs. He slapped another pair around Valah's ankles.

"Will that hold him?" asked Agorius.

"I hope so" replied Srisk.

The injured warrior grabbed the Ecclesiarch's outstretched hand and pulled himself up.

"How did he do all of that? He has no armour."

"I would assume that is why the Noxvata want him so badly." said Srisk. The Ecclesiarch opened a Recit channel.

"Liktus. Report"

"Holding steady just off the bridge Master. It's chaos out here. The Baron's forces have the upper hand. We don't have long."

"And Ortig?"

"Already have him Master. He's in the hold."

"Good. Let's get out of here."

*

The stolen bomber slid unnoticed from the burning cruiser carcass as the last of the Church of the Raven fighters were destroyed. There was catastrophic damage to the Dawn of Light and yet more explosions continued to mark its grey skin but the massive star ship was not completely finished. There was a high chance it would survive to sail again but for now the incapacitating damage had been the removal of its leader, Baron Valah.

He had regained his senses and knelt in the spacious hold of the commandeered bomber. Liktus had fashioned a rudimentary but effective containment cage that frequently crackled as blue sparks jumped from bar to bar.

Seelia had stripped her rifle and was painstakingly cleaning each component. Ortig too, was cleaning. He had found a small brush and was removing the blood, flesh and offal from the fissures in his stone skin. Srisk had joined Liktus in the cockpit on their long journey back to the Ninth Cloud.

The only member of the team that was not as relaxed was Agorius. He sat only a short distance from the Baron's cage. He had stitched the wound in his shoulder and applied a makeshift plasteel patch to his armour. He was settled on a supply crate with a plasma rifle laid across his thighs. He ran a gauntleted hand over his tattooed scalp as he fixed his gaze on the recovering Baron.

Agorius smiled as they locked eyes.

"You didn't see that coming did you?" he goaded.

"No I did not. The Ecclesiarch did his homework. He is to be applauded. He found my weakness but I will learn from that"

"Arrogance is the downfall of many a great leader" continued Agorius.

"And your kind would know I'm sure. There has never been a more arrogant race. Theocentricus. Centre of the galaxy." The Baron laughed.

A beep sounded on Agorius's feed. It was a message from Seelia. He looked over to her but she continued to clean her rifle. He opened the text.

[Srisk said explicitly not to talk to him]

Agorius ignored the note.

"At least I have not betrayed my own people. Your own sister wants you dead. What does that say about your mighty civilisation?"

"My sister has poisoned my people. If you knew what she had planned then it would be her that you'd have sitting in this cage. Besides, are you not considered a traitor on your world? The disgraced Centurio that no-one will follow. Tell me exactly how many soldiers have died under your command?"

Agorius stood up and took a step towards the cage.

"I have sacrificed much. I carry the death of every Optio-Immunis I have ever served with on my soul. You know nothing of service or honour."

"Call it whatever gives you peace of mind. You are an outcast, a failure, an abandoned wretch who now hides in the shadows and follows the orders of a puppeteer he neither knows or understands."

Agorius moved closer to the cage. Valah stood to meet his gaze.

"I'm sure an autopsy of your dead body would be enough for the Noxvata."

Agorius was about to raise his gun when the Baron's hand darted out between the bars and grabbed him by the throat.

"Let's settle this elsewhere" growled Valah.

Agorius was in shock, he saw coloured lights illuminate beneath the Baron's skin and then everything went black.

Seelia jumped from her seat and ran to the empty cage. There was no sign of the Baron or Agorius.

"I'm not telling the Ecclesiarch" said Ortig as he nervously fiddled with his knitting needles.

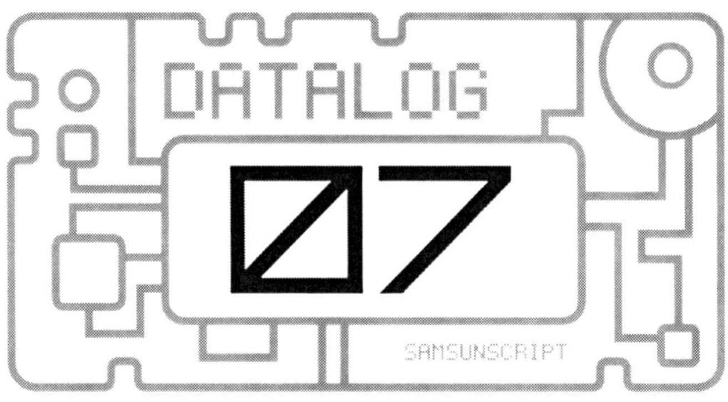

Solaris

"What happened?" demanded Srisk.

"It wasn't my fault" moaned Ortig.

The Ecclesiarch examined the empty cage. There were no signs of a struggle or that either Agorius or Valah had been there at all. Srisk's head-up display beeped.

[They were arguing. Valah reached through the cage, he had slipped his cuffs somehow. The air pressure intensified and then they just vanished.]

"Liktus. Get me the position of Agorius's locator beacon."

"Yes Master."

There was a moment's silence as Srisk strutted impatiently around the anomaly.

"Master?"

"Report."

"If I'm reading this correctly, the beacon is showing him in the Solaris star system."

"How can that be? That's over three light years away."

"I have a theory" suggested Liktus.

"Let's hear it."

"There is an entire panel on this bomber's console similar in setup to the ones I have seen on the stellar jump gates. I would guess the Baron has found a way to use folding technology on a much smaller scale."

[Do you mean he can jump across space?] The question came from Seelia.

"I believe he can" answered Liktus.

"If that is the case then perhaps as you suggest this ship has the same capability. Work it out quickly Liktus. We cannot lose him again."

"Is everything okay?" asked Ortig.

"No my friend. I fear the situation may get a lot worse before this is over."

Ortig looked as shocked as his limited facial expressions would allow.

"But you always tell me that things are going to be alright."

"That's because I believe it to be so. Now that we have learned that an individual can blink-travel, things have changed. The galaxy has changed. No my friend, this is not good at all."

*

Aleksy sat on the curb outside his semi-detached home. It was early in May and the morning sun warmed his bare legs. He lent back on his elbows and then adjusted his baseball cap to keep the bright sunlight from his eyes. He heard the front door slam shut behind him and then the garage door creak upward.

The noise of a car purred into life and he looked up as it reversed down the short driveway. The electric window hummed and the smiling familiar face of his foster father looked out.

"What time is Raff picking you up?"

"Nine" replied Aleksy

"He's late then?"

Aleksy nodded lethargically. It was a nice day, he didn't care.

"Well, have a great time and don't forget mum is cooking tea for five thirty."

"Yea I'll be back by then."

The tinted window slid back up and Aleksy watched the car as it left the cul-de-sac. It was another fifteen minutes before the clatter and cloud of grey smoke signalled the appearance of his friend's worn out Transit van. Aleksy watched as the vehicle drove over the corner of a low curb and then just brushed the wing mirror of his neighbour's car. Aleksy shook his head and smiled. He had been friends with Ralph since primary school. He had always had a reckless if not careless attitude to life. Ralph slid from the cab and bounded around the bonnet. He punched Aleksy's outstretched fist.

"Alek, how is it?"

"You're late Raff."

"Yea sorry. Had to stop to get some MacDee's plus the bike wouldn't start. Time for a new one."

Ralph said that all the time. If something didn't work as it should, he would have gladly thrown it away and bought a new one. The only trouble with that was he was as broke as Aleksy. The real reason that nothing of Ralph's worked properly was that he never looked after any of it.

"Your bike looks spotless. You been cleaning it with a toothbrush again?" asked Ralph.

"No course I haven't" lied Aleksy. "Come on give me a hand getting it in the van."

With both enduro motorbikes loaded and barely secured, Aleksy grabbed his open-faced helmet and the rest of his gear and jumped into the van. He took his motocross gloves from his holdall and shoved them into a large hole in the seat foam.

"When are you going to fix this seat?"

"Stop whining. This beauty has taken us all over the country."

Ralph patted the dirt caked dashboard and dust particles filled the air.

"This thing is held together with gaffer tape. I've no idea how it makes it anywhere."

"Similar to your KTM then?" replied Ralph.

"Ha, yeah true" agreed Aleksy. "Do you know where we are going? I have it marked on the O/S map, and have a rough postcode I could put into the sat-nav if you like."

"That's okay. I've been there with Frond and his mates a couple of times. Takes about forty minutes to get there. It's a cracking ride. The track follows an old drove all the way into Salisbury."

"Cool. Fingers crossed the bikes start!"

Aleksy handed his friend a half opened packet of mints.

"Cheers mate. Put some tunes on will ya."

Aleksy fiddled with the antiquated audio equipment. There was a cassette tape stuck halfway out of the player. He tried to remove it but it was clear that the tape had somehow unwound and was now stuck fast.

"Radio it is then" he smiled.

The two friends continued the journey without speaking for a while. Aleksy was staring out of the window wistfully daydreaming, while Ralph tapped his fingers on the steering wheel and whistled out of tune to the songs on the radio.

"I'm going to head down the pub after we get back. There's some skittles competition on or something. You fancy it?" asked Ralph.

"When are you going to clean your bike?"

"Not today that's for sure" laughed Ralph.

Aleksy raised his eyebrows.

"I'd love to, but it's my sister's birthday. I promised I'd be home for tea. Dad will do his nut if I'm not there."

"But you hate your sister."

"I don't hate her. She's just annoying."

"Well she's twelve. You were bloody annoying at that age too."

"Pot and Kettle" said Aleksy.

Ralph laughed.

"Are the relatives from Poland coming over?"

"I doubt it. Dad doesn't mention them too much. Only ever see them at a wedding or a funeral."

"Well no worries, if you can get away later, then come on down."

Aleksy looked back out of the sticker-clad side window. He often wondered about his family. His real family. He had been adopted when he was two. His foster father had divorced and then remarried his current wife thirteen years ago. He couldn't remember much of his first mother and knew absolutely nothing about his birth parents. He had asked, but his father was reluctant to talk about it so he hadn't pushed the matter. Besides he had done a great job bringing him up and providing for him. His step mother tried really hard and was genuinely a good person, it was just his step sister that annoyed him.

Just as Ralph had predicted it took them forty minutes to reach the picnic spot high on top of the hill. The dog walkers and ramblers all gave the pair a wide berth as they unloaded their motorbikes. A few more scowls and mumbled dissent could be heard before Ralph finally kicked over his bike. The four stroke engine had a meaty growl as well as a worrying knocking sound. It didn't seem to bother Ralph. Aleksy's bike was a few years newer. It had an electric start much to his friend's irritation. His dad had helped him buy it for his twenty-first birthday. That was four years ago and the trusty orange machine was still going strong. That was due in no small amount to the care and attention that Aleksy lavished upon it. There was no way he would leave his bike covered in mud after a ride out.

Aleksy tapped the waterproof button on his sat-map and the red route he had pre-programmed showed up as an overlay on the topographical display. He checked his pocket for the backup paper map.

"We all good?" asked Ralph slipping his mirrored goggles into place.

"Yes, sorted. Let's go."

"This is going to be a great ride. Try and keep up."

Ralph opened the throttle and the aggressive rear tyre dug into the gravel of the car park peppering Aleksy with roost.

*

Agorius woke. He was lying in a field of tall grass. The sweet smell was almost intoxicating. He moved his head slowly and then squinted as bright light stung his eyes. He moved again and an acute pain shot up his right leg. He turned his vambrace over and flipped up the cover to his suit controls. He tapped a button and ran a diagnostic. His suit was all working fine apart from his right leg. The servo's were damaged and the small screen alerted him to bone breakage. He had cracked his tibia and fibula. He surmised he had fallen from quite some height. His leg had taken the brunt of the trauma.

A few button presses later and a potent cocktail of medication was being pumped into his system. He grimaced as he tried to stand.

Just a short distance away the scarlet clad Baron was dusting grass seed from his tunic. He turned to look at Agorius.

"You made it also? That's a shame I was hoping you might have disintegrated during the journey."

Agorius grabbed the baton attached to his thigh and triggered the luminous head.

"What have you done?"

"It is the next step in evolution. We have managed to combine technology with our own physiology."

"That is nothing new."

"Oh but it is. Your crude suit is an addition to your frail body. Even now I expect it is pumping you full of drugs. What I possess is something very different. It is a part of me. It can change my atomic structure, and as you can see I am able to blink-travel. I must admit this is the first field trial if you'll forgive the pun."

Agorius moved his weight from his broken leg and scanned the background.

"Where are we?"

The Baron span around. He seemed completely uninjured.

"I confess I do not know. I was unable to program a location due to my restrictions. So this would be a random habitable planet from my database. If you give me a moment I will tell you exactly."

Agorius moved towards the Baron and raised his light hammer.

"I don't care where we are I'm going to smash that smug head of yours into a pulp."

"Wait!" insisted the Baron. "At least hear what I have to say."

"Why should I?" grunted Agorius.

"Please do not misunderstand me ex-Centurio, I will happily fight and kill you, but you should know why my sister wants me captured."

"Because you're a traitor."

"On the contrary. I would save my people from the bloodshed she and those of her cabal have planned."

"Go on" said Agorius suspiciously.

"I discovered a plot that was instigated by my father. They desire a return to war with the Moretti."

"Why would anyone want such a thing? We are at peace."

"For the moment we are. The Moretti have ceased hostilities because their holy leader the 'Paragon' died. They are in mourning. When they choose a new principal they will continue where they left off. None of us are sure when that will be, maybe a year maybe a thousand years. My sister wants to attack them first, to mobilise the armies of the Federation and make the first strike. To aid them she wants the folding technology I have developed for my fleet. That is why she and the Noxvata want me."

"It makes sense to attack first. We could push them back. Retake those worlds that fell under their yoke."

"We could, but even with this capability millions would die. There is another way."

"And you're going to tell me what that is I presume."

The Baron ignored the jibe.

"If the Moretti will only fight when a leader is appointed then that is their weakness. We can exploit it. Instead of our armies smashing against each other we can jump into the heart of their civilisation and remove the Paragon. Once we return his head they will mourn afresh. Eventually they will have no choice but to abandon their quest for this galaxy."

Agorius ran his hand over his scalp.

"That makes sense. So why haven't you told your sister of your plan?"

"Oh I have. There is another reason why they seek a return to war."

"What is that?"

"Money and power. In a time of relative peace there is no need to buy arms or the latest defence technology, and in case you weren't aware that is what Households of Keterus economies rely on. We are a resourceful people and I am sure we could find new avenues for our skills, but with those current house leaders losing billions with every passing crescent, I would imagine they require a more time bound solution. As for your masters, the Noxvata. What use are they now? If indeed they held the balance between the Federation and Moretti during the war, then what power do they have in this time of peace. Their influence wanes as does their secretive agenda. They would only benefit from a return to hostilities."

"And you, the Baron of one of those very households would give up your birthright, cripple your world's finances in order to save lives. I don't buy it" snorted Agorius. Valah's skin on his left arm glowed and the Baron looked down at it. The real motives of the vain Baron then crawled into Agorius's mind.

"You seek to be the one who would save the galaxy" stated Agorius. "The one who would save millions of lives. The great Baron Valah, the one who would vanquish the Moretti Paragon. The one who can fold space."

"Is that so bad?" smiled Valah.

"No one man should have that much power. It's not the folding technology of your fleet that the Noxvata want, it is you. It is your ability to blink-travel."

"Well until a moment ago, that was unproven." The Baron looked at his arm once again. The skin glowed. "Your friends are nothing if not persistent. They will be with us shortly. As much as I am enjoying this conversation ex-Centurio I think it is time for me to leave, I have a battle-cruiser to repair."

"Running again?" taunted Agorius. He moved the light hammer in his hand. "Perhaps you should stay and tell the Ecclesiarch your little story."

"You really are nothing but a mindless primate. Perhaps a return war would be a good thing as it would be mostly your kind dying on the front line."

The Baron jumped back as the blinding light of the hammer head slapped into the soft earth. Valah smiled.

"I guess I have time before I go."

The Baron spun in the air like he had been unleashed from a gyroscopic toy. He landed behind Agorius and thrust out a kick into his lower back. The power of the blow cracked Agorius's amour and sent him flying more than ten metres across the green field. Before he could right himself he felt the Baron land on his back. Warning lights bleeped and flashed as Valah pummelled his bare fists into the power plant of Agorius's suit. The ex-Centurio managed to turn and elbow Valah in the shoulder. It was enough to dislodge him.

Agorius gritted his teeth as his broken leg took his weight as he stood. He raised his forearm to protect himself from the Baron's strike. The unprotected fist of Valah smashed the control unit on his arm. All signals from his battle suit were lost. The armour still functioned but Agorius had no idea for how long. He brought the light hammer up smashing into Valah's midriff. Agorius pushed forward using the sparking hammer head like a battering ram. He then span the weapon and with all his might trying to pulverise the Baron's head.

Valah used both his arms to form a cross block. His fingers curled around the haft and then he sent out another formidable front kick. Agorius tumbled backwards minus his light hammer. He glanced down at his abdominal plating. It was cracked and hydraulic liquid oozed from the fissure. He looked up to see Valah throw his hammer into the undergrowth.

"So antiquated" laughed the Baron.

Agorius tapped the underside of each forearm and two serrated blades shot out over his fists. One crackled with power the other only reflected the light. Agorius surged forward. He blocked and then struck back with a lifetime of training. The Baron held the upper hand with his unnatural shielding abilities, but Agorius was born to fight.

The frenzied attack was slowly wearing down the invisible field that protected Valah. A trickle of blood ran down the left side of his neck and there was a deeper tear across his stomach. The material of his tunic had soaked up the blood and had stuck to his skin.

Agorius was also struggling. Both legs were in pain and his suit was failing. There were multiple cracks in his plating and he was coated in purple and green fluid from the waist down. His movements slowed with each attack. It wouldn't be long before his life-giving battle suit became a metal coffin.

Agorius batted away a strike from the Baron and reached out with his left arm. His metal gauntlet clamped around Valah's neck. Agorius urged the servos on his fingers to close. At the same time he rammed the blades on his right fist towards Valah's heart. The motors in his arms and shoulders whined as Agorius sought to push the blades through the shield. The Baron struck out in desperation as he felt the cold tip of the long metal claws touch his flesh. The Baron's blows battered Agorius's scalp until the white of bone stared through. Yet still the determined warrior would not release his grip. The twin blades dug deeper and Valah cried out for the first time. The Baron saw the glee in the eyes of the ex-Centurio and in that moment knew that he would not win this battle of wills.

He rolled backwards and twisted his body. The blades of Agorius tore into his chest but missed his heart. The Baron landed on his back. He folded his legs and then uncurled them like a spring, catapulting Agorius over his head.

*

Aleksy scanned the route ahead. It was a poor choice of lines. They were all ruts. Ralph had headed down the middle. Chunks of turf were scuffed away where the bike's foot pegs had hit them due to the deeper sections. It hadn't bothered Ralph he was stood up whooping as his tyres bounced off the dirt troughs. Aleksy took the higher route to the right. He let the handlebars bounce towards his stomach as a short succession of bumps threatening to throw him off. The back end went light as he leaned forward and his rear tyre slid into the central rut. He would have to follow Ralph now.

Despite the difficult riding Aleksy had a smile that filled his open faced helmet. He had dropped his goggles to his chest as they were caked in mud so he held back slightly from his friend not wanting to get an eyeful of dirt.

The track opened up into a long straight and it looked as if it had been recently resurfaced. The grey shale was a usual giveaway sign. Local four wheel drive groups or organisations such as the TRF were usually responsible for the trail's upkeep as well as its destruction. Ralph created a dust cloud which filled the track. The particles were kept from escaping by the overhanging tree canopies. Aleksy headed in blind. If there was anything in the way he wouldn't be able to avoid it.

He sailed through and out into a less dusty area. Ahead the trail was completely submerged. Even in summer the water would congregate in certain pockets. There were tyres marks on either side of the track where some riders had chosen to avoid the water obstacle. Ralph had lifted his front wheel into a low wheelie and plummeted through it. As it turned out it wasn't that deep. Aleksy followed suit, standing, to try and avoid most of the initial splash. Water filled his boots and steam billowed from his hot exhaust and engine.

As Aleksy left the large puddle his bike skidded sideways but he managed to shift his weight and stop it from falling. His heart hammered in his chest and the buzz of adrenaline made his muscles momentarily tense. He breathed out deeply and watched Ralph and his machine expertly leap from a rounded hump. He landed some distance away and then slowed down. Aleksy could see Ralph turn his head ready to watch his attempt at a jump. Aleksy was a good rider but he never felt safe when both tyres left the ground. It always seemed like he was metres in the air when actually he was only a few inches. He gritted his teeth and opened the throttle. As his front wheel touched the crest he watched in disbelief as a hulking figure smashed into Ralph and his bike.

Aleksy lost all concentration and his bike nose dived. The force threw him over the handlebars and his bike somersaulted over his head. Dust filled his vision. He could hear his bike's engine roar and then the crunching of metal as it hit the ground again. Luckily his body armour and in particular his spine protector had saved him from serious injury. He wiped his eyes as he stood up.

The scene in front of him was unreal. His brain could not decipher what he was witnessing. Lying in the track was a massive creature. It looked to be wearing armour, but most of that was cracked or broken. There was barbed wire wrapped around its legs where it had crashed through the fence. It had no nose, just two slits and markings over its head and under one of its yellow eyes. It looked in pain. A smaller man dressed in a crimson tunic was walking towards it. He looked human but was obviously injured as he held one hand to his side.

Ralph's bike was partly obscured under the giant creature, the front wheel almost bent into a right angle. Ralph had removed his helmet and was also trying to understand what he was seeing. He shouted something at the man in crimson and moved towards him. His bike was mashed, he wasn't happy. The bizarre nature of the situation seemed lost on him. He continued to curse at the tall robed individual. Aleksy watched as the man struck out towards his friend. Ralph doubled over and cried out in pain. With another swift movement the strange newcomer grabbed the back of Ralph's body armour and threw him up the track. It was as if Ralph had been a mere inconvenience. Aleksy rushed towards his friend. He was lying face down on the stone strewn track.

Aleksy flipped him over.

"Raff! Raff are you okay?"

Ralph's eyes were open but they stared blankly out into space. Aleksy looked down and then had to stop himself from being sick. He urged again but could not look away from the gaping hole in his friend's chest. It was the smell that finally made him turn his head.

Further down the track he watched as the crimson robed man knelt on the giant creature's chest and continued to punch downwards. He was like a machine and his fists were like pistons beating the armoured thing to a pulp. Anger swam swiftly through Aleksy's veins and a red haze blotted out the sunlight. As he stood he picked up a long section of angled steel that had been used as a makeshift fence post. He pulled the remnants of barbed wire from it and ran.

Aleksy jumped high into the air and with both hands around the metal stave he drove it through the kneeling man's back. Only as he fell to the side and saw the bloody tip protruding from the front of the man's chest did he realise what he had done. The man sagged forwards and coughed blood onto the shattered armoured torso upon which he was sat. He slowly turned his head towards Aleksy. His eyes burned with hatred.

"I'm sorry" pleaded Aleksy.

He tried to scrabble back along the track but the tall robed man grabbed his boot. Even with the steel stake through his body he managed to pull Aleksy towards him. He fought to free himself, but the man's vice-like grip just pulled him nearer. Aleksy looked at the jagged spike sticking from the man's chest. He was sure he was going to be pulled onto it. The bloody tip touched his plastic breastplate and the strange man looked deep into his eyes.

"Do not trust them." The words sounded rehearsed, over dramatic.

"Who?" stuttered Aleksy.

"Do not waste this gift."

With that the man flung his head back and a glowing ball of light rose from his open mouth. All colour drained from his body and his grip loosened. Aleksy watched mesmerised as the white sphere hovered in mid air. He could see tiny tendrils writhe around its surface like living fibre optic filaments. Suddenly Aleksy gulped as the ball dove down his throat. He fell backwards coughing, scratching at his neck. He felt a warm sensation spread from his gut and his limbs started to tingle. He held his hand aloft and worry framed his face as he watched his skin undulate like hundreds of worms crawled beneath the surface. The light faded to black and Aleksy passed out.

*

Voices woke him. He opened his eyes. He was amazed he was still alive. He stared up into two captivating eyes. They were behind a blue glass visor and the woman's skin looked as if it was silver. She was wearing over-the-ear headphones.

"Help me?" pleaded Aleksy

The woman turned her head. Aleksy couldn't hear her say anything but almost instantly there came a reply from a short distance away.

"No!"

As the silver skinned woman moved to one side Aleksy pulled himself up. Towering over the bodies stood a cloaked figure and behind him was what looked like a stone gorilla only twice the size.

"I will need to delve into his mind. He may have witnessed what happened here."

"Delve into whose mind?" said Aleksy.

The hooded figure looked directly at Aleksy. The intense orange of his eyes burned brighter.

"You can understand me?" asked the tall figure.

Aleksy nodded.

"Strange. Tell me Terran what happened here?"

Aleksy looked back up the track to where Ralph lay motionless. The tall creature followed his gaze.

"He was your friend?"

"Yes" replied Aleksy.

"I am sorry for your loss. This should not have happened."

"What, should not have happened? Who are you people? And why is he dressed in that costume? Are you from the circus or something?"

"My name is Ecclesiarch Srisk. This is Seelia and that creature over there is called Ortig. This one lying here is our dead colleague Agorius."

"What about him?" Aleksy pointed at the body of the crimson clad man. He was bent double.

"His name was Valah. He is the reason we are here."

"He is the one that killed my friend." A tear started to form in Aleksy's eye.

"Tell me what happened" asked Srisk.

Aleksy quickly regaled the story whilst wiping the tear from his eye.

"You killed Valah?" asked Srisk clearly stunned.

"It was self defence" said Aleksy.

"What? A stake through the back?" replied Srisk.

"We should call the police. This is not right. I have no idea what's going on." protested Aleksy.

Aleksy unzipped his jacket pocket and took out his mobile phone.

"That would not be wise" suggested Srisk. The Ecclesiarch tapped on his forearm.

Aleksy looked at his phone. There was no signal.

"What is your name Terran?" enquired Srisk.

"I am Aleksy. Aleksy Black. Everyone calls me Alek, and what do you mean Terran?"

"Well Alek, let me be brief as we don't have much time. We call this world Terra, therefore you are a Terran. As you may have surmised we are not from this planet."

"Aliens?" Aleksy smiled.

"To you, I would suppose we are" agreed Srisk.

All of the colour drained from Aleksy's face. He had been thinking it, but his rational self had denied it as a possibility. His mind swam. He couldn't focus. What was he going to tell his father?

"Your father?" The question came from the hooded Ecclesiarch.

"How did you...? You can read minds?"

"Some thoughts shout out to me that is all" said Srisk.

"I have to get back" said Aleksy shaking his head. "I have to tell Ralph's parents what happening. What am I going to say?"

"I am afraid I cannot allow that" said Srisk solemnly.

"What do you mean you can't allow it?" demanded Aleksy.

"Our presence here is a violation. We must leave immediately. All traces of our time in this world must be erased."

Aleksy stood open mouthed as Ortig picked up the two smaller bodies under one arm and then grabbed the foot of Agorius's corpse and started to drag them out into the field. Seelia picked up Ralph's crumpled bike and hoisted it onto her shoulder. Aleksy was amazed she could even lift it.

"You have a choice Alek Black" said Srisk. "Your first journey ends here. It is up to you whether you desire to start another."

"You mean I have to come with you? What, do you have a spaceship or something?"

Srisk turned his head back to the field where Ortig and Seelia suddenly vanished. The air around them rippled like quicksilver and the vast expanse of the Keteran bomber slowly revealed itself.

"Oh my God" said Aleksy. He looked up into the Ecclesiarch's dark cowl.

"What if I cannot? What about my dad?"

"You already know the answers to those questions Alek."

The Ecclesiarch walked over to Aleksy's motorbike and plucked it from the ground like it was made of plastic.

"Are you coming?"

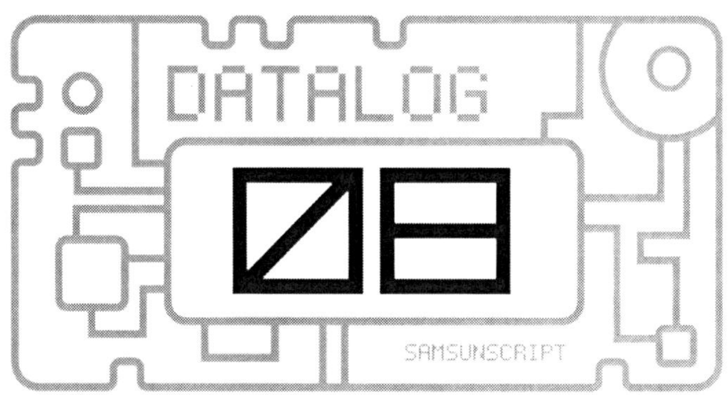

Desolation

Aleksy looked out of the small octagonal window. His breath misted a small circular patch on the trans-glass. He marked two dots with his fingertip and then drew a smile underneath. The blue planet he had left behind looked almost fragile.

He still couldn't believe where he was or what had happened. Scenarios replayed over and over in his mind like the repeated shows he once watched on television. They were never this sad.

He felt a heavy hand on his shoulder.

"One day your world may join the Federation. You would be able to return." Srisk's tone of voice was measured and practical.

"They will never know" sighed Aleksy.

"What do you mean?"

"My parents, my family, my friends even my annoying sister. None of them will ever know what happened to me and to Raff. Pictures of us will appear on Facebook asking if people have seen us."

"What is Facebook?"

"It doesn't matter." Aleksy shook his head and then turned to look at the cloaked Ecclesiarch. "What matters is that I know Raff is dead. I can mourn him. His family can't. They can't move on and neither can the people that know me. Are you sure there is no way I can contact them? Just to let them know I am safe. I won't say anything else I promise."

"What would you say?" answered Srisk.

"That I am moving away, that I am going to spend some time travelling and that I would contact them when I could, but not for them to worry." Aleksy looked hopeful.

"What about your friend's death?" probed Srisk. "What would you say about that?"

"Perhaps it's better that they think him alive. Isn't it? I could say he's with me."

"But he is not. He can never return" stated Srisk.

"So what are you saying?"

"These will be difficult times for all those you loved and that loved you. Maybe you will return one day, maybe you will not. But they can always hope that you will. Do you honestly believe your father would swallow the story of you both leaving without a word?"

"No he wouldn't, but why can't I tell him the truth?" asked Aleksy.

"For the very same reason, plus I cannot allow it. I have done many regrettable things in my long life but I will not alter the future of an entire civilisation. Terra is a category three planet. Your world is not ready to join the Federation. We broke every contact law conceivable just being there. Your situation is unfortunate, but you are still alive. It is time to look forward and to pack your memories away, for the moment at least."

"You make that sound very easy." Aleksy managed a thin smile.

"Believe me Alek Black it is not. Time only dulls the edges, it does not make you forget."

Aleksy looked across the wide space at the covered bodies and the two motorbikes.

"What will happen to him?"

"You can perform whatever rites are appropriate for your culture just as soon as we arrive."

"Arrive where?"

<Yes Srisk. Where?> The thought stamped into the Ecclesiarch's mind.

The Ecclesiarch clanked to the bulkhead of the bomb bay.

"Liktus. Pull me up a map on this display."

He turned to the others.

"This is a time of change for us all. Forgive me Alek but not all of this will make sense. I promise to explain in detail, en route." Aleksy nodded. "We failed in our mission to bring back the Baron and lost one of our own in the process. Whatever usefulness we once offered to the Noxvata I think has expired. I had my doubts about this mission from the outset. It was as if they just wanted us out of the way."

"Out of the way for what?" asked Ortig.

"I do not know, but perhaps it is time we found out." Srisk looked at each of them. A message bleeped on the map screen behind him. It was from Seelia.

[We're listening.]

"I would guess that the Noxvata and the Houses of Keterus were after the folding technology that the Baron has developed. What they intend to do with it is what we need to discover. Perhaps if we reveal the end game, then there may be a route back for all of us in the eyes of the Noxvata. Or at the very least clarity."

"I don't understand" admitted Ortig.

"Me neither" said Aleksy flippantly.

Seelia cast him a stern glance.

"I propose that we travel to Keterus-Alpha and politely ask the Baroness about her agreement with the Noxvata. We have the folding technology. Maybe we have something to offer. Whatever the case I would like to know the truth."

"Okay. Still don't understand" said Ortig "But I'm in."

Seelia nodded. Aleksy looked blankly at the star map.

"I wasn't aware I had a choice."

Srisk ignored him and pointed to a spot on the holographic display.

"We need to change craft. This bomber will provoke too many questions when we enter the Cursus system. I suggest we land here in the Khufu Asteroid Belt and exchange it for something more suitable to our new found situation. Liktus can remove the blink drive. There are more pirates in this sector than anywhere else in the galaxy so we should be right at home. Any questions?"

Aleksy put his hand in the air and then immediately put it down again.

"Who are the Noxvata?" he asked.

Srisk ignored the question. He looked directly at Aleksy but his next question was directed at Liktus over the Recit.

"What did you discover on the Baron's autopsy?"

"Nothing Master. His physiology was unchanged."

"There was nothing left at the landing site?"

"Not that I could detect. I scanned a wide area on all frequencies" replied Liktus.

"That leaves us with a puzzle." Srisk was still staring at the human. Aleksy fidgeted under his gaze. "How did Valah travel? And where is the equipment he used?" There was a moment's silence.

"I don't know" pleaded Aleksy. "I've told you what happened. I can't remember all of it."

"You did. It still does not explain how you are able to understand us without any aural implant or translation device."

"I thought you all spoke my language." The statement was genuine, but Seelia couldn't help sniggering. "Well at least I talk" declared Aleksy. "You haven't said a word since I met you."

Seelia glared back and then turned to walk away.

"What's her problem?" asked Aleksy

"She chooses not to speak. It is her way. I will find you a suit that has a communication console. Then you can talk to her, although there is no guarantee she will reply. You have much to learn Terran. Come with me, I will fill you in on the ten thousand years of history you are missing."

*

The Khufu Asteroid belt was vast. Seen from a distance it resembled a bucking nebula but on closer inspection it revealed millions of rocks. Some smaller than a drop pod others large enough to be classified as proto-planets. The ever moving entity made it virtually impossible to map, which also made it a favoured haunt for all those wishing to avoid the eye of the Agency or the Federation.

One such planetoid of immorality was Sojun's Peak. It occupied a large asteroid with an abnormally large mountain pinnacle. It was one of the more easy to recognise locations. To that end it was often the first port of call for those entering the belt. The majority of the useable land was piled high with ships of every size and shape. It was a colossal breaker's yard.

Huddled at the foot of Sojun's Peak was a small but energetic hab complex. There were numerous Restols that catered for the passing throng and then the more salubrious establishments that served liquor, took bets or provided any number of deviant comforts. It was a melting pot of cultures and races that didn't ask questions as long as your credit was sound.

Liktus had landed the state-of-the-art bomber away from the central landing zone on Srisk's instructions. The Ecclesiarch and Seelia had left to broker a deal on exchanging the ship whilst Liktus set about the removal of the blink-drive. Aleksy was trying to recall the supply list on his new suit's data-log. Srisk had sent him into the hab complex with strict instructions. He was accompanied by Ortig who had seemed reluctant to leave the bomb bay.

Aleksy's head hurt. He was still trying to digest the information the Ecclesiarch had overloaded him with. Only the day before he had been playing basketball and eating pizza. Now here he was bouncing along in an enviro suit on a low gravity asteroid light years from home. Surreal was the only word that kept ricocheting through his mind.

The pair reached an airlock. One of the yellow warning lights was broken and the other flashed intermittently. Aleksy held his hand to the entry pad and the doors slowly opened. The pressure equalisation alert bonged green and the inner doors opened. Aleksy pressed the sensor on the side of his helmet and the visor slid back. He breathed deeply expecting a fresh intake of clean air but immediately coughed as the stale, almost smoky artificial atmosphere, clogged his lungs. He turned to Ortig who was pulling a wheeled crate.

"How come you don't need breathing equipment?" asked Aleksy.

"I dunno" replied Ortig.

"Where are you from?" he continued.

"Not sure" said Ortig.

"You can't remember or you don't know?"

"Not sure" repeated Ortig.

"I guess it doesn't matter" said Aleksy jovially. "What about that collar. What does it do?"

"You ask lots of questions" stated Ortig.

"Yea, I'm sorry. Everything is still so new to me. I really can't believe I'm here. If I'm being honest it's all a bit of a struggle. I'm just trying to keep myself occupied to stop myself from going mad."

"Mad!" said Ortig. He tapped the collar.

"What do you mean?" inquired Aleksy.

"Srisk says that the collar stops me going mad."

"How much do you know about him? Srisk I mean." asked Aleksy.

"Not much" shrugged Ortig.

"Well I'm glad you're with me, you know in case we get in any trouble. This place looks like a slum."

"I don't want any trouble" said Ortig quickly. He seemed somewhat distressed.

"No, me neither" assured Aleksy. "I was just saying if we do, it's good to know you've got my back."

"I do not want your back" said Ortig confused.

"Yeah okay. Let's just get the supplies" conceded Aleksy.

*

Srisk watched as the squat Hoigen looked around the Keteran bomber. His name was Atlar. He was the person you had to deal with on all matters concerning the breaker's yard. He wore a faded orange enviro suit that had patches glued all over it. Even his spherical glass helmet had cracks that were taped. He ran his stubby fingers along the landing gear of the ship and then returned to Srisk and Seelia.

"She's lovely" said Atlar.

"What's it worth?" asked Srisk.

"Ah well now, loveliness doesn't necessarily mean expensiveness does it? Besides why would you be wanting to sell her? You've seen the quality of the ships I have here. Some of 'em don't even have density drives. Are you sure this is yours to sell?"

"Can you see anyone else here claiming it?" replied Srisk.

"Well that's a fair point. Still I'm thinking she's a bit on the hot side. Not sure I can move her on as she is. May have to break it for bits. Be a shame, she is lovely."

"What you do with it is your decision. I will need a replacement ship. Something with speed, good shielding and armed."

"Oh is that all?" smiled Atlar.

"Of course I'll need the difference credited to my slate" insisted Srisk.

"Difference?" Atlar almost choked on the word. The thought of spending money made his light blue skin darken. "Follow me. I think I have something that I could do a deal on."

Srisk and Seelia followed the barrel-like Atlar through the artificial canyons of metal work. Indiscernible piles of equipment were stacked closely together. Some showed signs of plasma cutting where pieces had been scavenged. Others were complete vehicles. A few still had the scorch marks of their last encounter. Wires and endless miles of conduit snaked through the complex like arteries. It was a maze of machinery.

They walked into a moderate clearing and seated on top of an enormous de-tracked geo-rover was an ancient looking craft. It had symbols daubed across the main body like some random graffiti and its shield plating seemed to have more bullet holes than metal. The fuselage was long, boxy and thin. The cockpit was set back some distance from the nose and shielded by a metal canopy. The majority of the ship consisted of engine. Two huge faceted boxes were attached to the hull either side of the nose and two more were duplicated further back. They were currently vertical which allowed the craft to take off and land. Once in flight they would rotate parallel with the main body. There looked to be bits missing as well as huge oil stained tarpaulins covering some sections.

"Granted she's not a looker, and she isn't the fastest girl around but she's dependable."

Srisk's head-up display blipped.

[It's junk] typed Seelia.

"What is it? A tug?"asked Srisk.

"That it is. You have a good eye there. She is an early bird. Maybe even dates back to the second expansion. I'll be straight with you, she hasn't got density drives so she's a bit on the sluggish side but she was made to pull the jump gates out into uncharted space. So she's more powerful than a Giant Grull and got armour thicker than a Velamor's hide and sturdy shields to back 'em up. She's not lacking in the firepower department either. Turrets top and bottom, and some hefty chuggers under the chin. Appreciate it's not plasma but I'll load it up to the gills for you."

Atlar moved closer to Srisk and whispered.

"I'll even chuck in a couple of dirty boys. I hate having them things round here. I'm guessing you'll be able to make use of 'em."

"I'll take it" said Srisk.

Seelia put her hand on his arm and linked minds.

<If we get caught in a fire-fight, we are sitting ducks. I could run faster than this bucket.>

<True. But we have a blink drive. We need a bulldozer not a race-craft.>

"So you havin' it or what?" pressed Atlar.

"What's the price?" replied Srisk.

"Straight swap. And I'll throw in that ammo and the you know what." Atlar winked.

Srisk held out his hand and bumped his armoured knuckles against the Hoigen's fist.

"Deal."

Srisk turned to walk away and then stopped.

"One last thing. Does she have a name?"

Atlar chuckled.

"Yea, she's called the 'Desolation'."

*

Aleksy sat with his head in his hands. They had been waiting for what seemed like an eternity for the store assistant to fill their crate. He had fiddled with the comms interface on his suit hoping to find a game of some description but was disappointed to find only practical applications. He had mentioned to Ortig that 'it doesn't even have snake', but the stone behemoth was sound asleep and rumbling like a distant thunderstorm.

Aleksy had sent several messages to Seelia, all with a humorous twist, at least that is how he had intended them. He eventually received a reply which read:

[Keep this channel clear. Priority comms only]

After counting all of the metal studs on the counter-front, working out the percentage of cracked tiles versus whole ones on the floor and daring himself to touch Ortig's collar Aleksy was thoroughly bored. He stood up and walked to the store counter. The rotund blue assistant was checking the readout against the stock piled up on their crate. He looked up as the human peered over.

"Nearly done. Just a few more items. There is a Restol just down the corridor. They have a bar. You could wait there. I'll let your friend know when this is ready."

"Now you tell me" muttered Aleksy under his breath.

He looked down the long gloomy corridor. Srisk had told him to stay at the supply hatch, but surely just a look wouldn't hurt.

Aleksy bounced down a set of creaking metal steps and into a wider communal area. There were various fluorescent avenues leading off from the central hub and lots of closed doors. It reminded Aleksy of a hotel wing except instead of wood the doorways were riveted steel and replacing the room number were small signs indicating the kind of establishment lurking behind it. The first one Aleksy came across read 'Urwin's Restol & Bar'. He nervously pushed open the door and stepped inside.

The place was dark. Aleksy wasn't sure whether that was the ambience the owners were trying to create or whether it was due to the many missing or broken light fixtures. Two glass doors blocked the way ahead but a small sign labelled 'bar' pointed to the right. Aleksy could hear the noise of conversation and smell that unmistakeable stale odour that accompanied most drinking establishments. The layout was a series of booths that formed a circle around the island bar.

Most of the patrons were Hoigen. The blue skin gave them away. There were a few other humanoid types but nothing spectacularly different. Aleksy had secretly expected a scene from the Mos Eisley Cantina. This certainly wasn't Star Wars, but it was real. He walked to the counter and picked up a digital slate. An animated character which Aleksy didn't recognise danced across the screen on top of the 'Urwin's' logo. He tapped the screen and a list of beverages appeared. Aleksy had no idea what any of them were. The bartender sat upon a gravity chair and nudged a joystick to bring himself in front of the newly arrived customer.

"What can I get for you?" he asked almost cheerfully.

Aleksy paused.

"Um, what do you recommend?" he asked.

"Well I aint drinking it boy, so how should I know?"

"I'm just not sure what everything is." admitted Aleksy

"Yea I can see you are new here. Well what do you want to achieve? Memory loss, all over body numbness, an energetic curve, what?"

"I just wanted to get a drink while I wait for my supplies to be sorted."

"Morgan's Malaise it is then."

The barman's chair span and he rattled a couple of the bottles that were forming the spirit display. He rotated back and slapped a small glass onto the counter. The black liquid inside slopped onto the metal top. Aleksy stared at the barman who silently stared back.

"Slate?" he said finally.

"Of course." Aleksy apologised and handed the barman the data-slate Srisk had given him. He swiped it and then passed it back. Aleksy took the drink and turned to find a seat. As he did he bumped into a tall grey skinned individual knocking his fizzing glass to the floor. Aleksy had seen his kind before. Srisk had called him Agorius. He was a Theo-something.

Before Aleksy could apologise for a second time the Theocentrican slapped the small shot glass from his hand and grabbed him around the throat. Aleksy felt his feet leave the floor.

"You'll pay for that" he growled.

"Of course" gurgled Aleksy. "I'll get my slate."

"That's not what I meant." The man's protruding brow furrowed.

Aleksy looked around the bar. He had expected to see all eyes on them but no-one was paying any attention. Even the barman seemed unfazed. The stout fingers around his throat started to close. Aleksy pushed the creeping panic from his mind and as he did so he felt a warmth in his arms. He held them up to see a subtle glow coming from beneath the skin.

Suddenly he punched upwards. His fist caught his attacker in the joint of his elbow. The Theocentrican's arm doubled and he released his hold. Aleksy's left arm came up by the side of his head blocking a roundhouse swing. The grey man stumbled backwards clutching his wrist as if he was in pain. Aleksy had felt nothing.

He watched as the tall Theocentrican drew a shiny knife from inside his jacket. He smiled as he rasped the edge against his square-cut chin. Moving with incredible speed the grey man shot forward. Aleksy turned his body just a fraction and the knife sailed harmless past his enviro-suit. In a blur of motion Aleksy grabbed the outstretched arm and reversed the strike bending the assailant's arm as he did so. He pushed up with his body and the keen blade stabbed the Theocentrican beneath his chin and up into his brain. Aleksy released his grip and then planting his feet firmly he brought his shoulders square and punched the burbling giant in the chest. The blow took the enormous ogre off his feet and flung him backwards. He skidded across the sticky floor before his head crashed into the base of one of the booths.

Aleksy stared down at his hands. The faint glow had gone. He looked around the bar. Not one soul looked up. A tapping came from the central island bar.

"Where did you learn to fight like that?" asked the bartender.

"I had two karate lessons when I was eight" replied Aleksy.

It was clear that the Hoigen didn't understand.

"Fair enough. That'll be a thousand credits."

"What for?"

"Unless you want to clean up the mess and dispose of the body yourself?"

"Oh No. Of course not." Aleksy handed his slate over once more and at the same time his comms unit sounded. He checked the message. It was from Srisk.

[Do you have the supplies?]

He took his data-slate from the barman and turned his back on Urwin's Restol and Bar. He typed as he walked.

[Ortig is with them.]

There was a long pause.

[Our new ride is being prepped. Meet me at my beacon location now. Can you remember how to do that?]

[Yes] tapped Aleksy.

*

By the time Aleksy had reached the Ecclesiarch he is was out of breath. The zigzag climb up the mountainside had proved more difficult than he had imagined, even with the low gravity and his suit supplying fresh oxygen. He had quickly understood the reason behind the summons. Lining the steep route up the slopes of Sojun's Peak were hundreds or circular stones inset into the rock face. Most had engraved names or plaques and some were adorned with keepsakes and trinkets. As Aleksy climbed higher there were a few that were missing their stone plugs revealing a clean cut circular bore hole. It was a strange kind of outdoor mausoleum.

Srisk was standing adjacent to a freshly sealed grave. There was a small metal plate that read: Centurio Agorius Millus. The Ecclesiarch indicated to the circular blank cap stone in front of Aleksy.

"I am not familiar with your customs when it comes to your dead. I hope this is agreeable?"

Aleksy picked up a small stone and leant forward. He scratch the letters R.A.F.F. into the smooth surface.

"This is fine." He looked back over the small hab centre and the vast expanse of derelict spacecraft. "It's very peaceful up here. I think Raff would have approved." Aleksy handed Srisk his data slate.

"Is everything okay?" asked the Ecclesiarch.

"Well, sort of" hesitated Aleksy.

Srisk scrolled through the entries on the device and then looked up.

"What happened?"

"I'm not sure" answered Aleksy honestly. "It all unfolded very quickly. I think I am still in shock. I knocked a drink out of his hand. He picked me up by the neck. The next thing I knew I had stabbed him in the throat and knocked him across the other side of the bar." He paused for a moment. "I killed him."

"Are you injured?"

"No" replied Aleksy. "Not a scratch."

"Then there is nothing to worry about."

"But he's dead."

"That was his choice. He decided to confront you, fate decided the outcome."

"What about the police? Won't somebody miss him?"

"Maybe. The Agency would be involved if we were on another world, but out here the law is unwritten and justice is served by those who live here. Is this only other life you have taken apart from the Baron?"

"Yea, that sort of thing is frowned upon back on Earth."

"How does it make you feel?" asked Srisk.

"I don't know. I don't really feel anything. Nothing seems real any more. I am still thinking one day I'll wake up and this will have been a very believable nightmare."

"You are coping with the transition well. I have seen minds crumble when they have been exposed to the reality of the universe outside of their own world."

"Perhaps my mind is not that complicated" smiled Aleksy.

The Ecclesiarch seemed to ignore the human's attempt at humour.

"It bodes well for our future plans. I am starting to think our meeting was destined."

"What about our future plans?" inquired Aleksy.

"Our trip to the House of Keterus. You are not too dissimilar to their lineage. You will be able to pass as one of them."

"I don't like the sound of this."

"It is our best play" assured Srisk. The Ecclesiarch reached out and placed his hand against Agorius's tomb door. "Sleep well my friend."

They started to walk back down the diagonal mountain path. Aleksy's mind raced. There was so much to process. He had always felt that he had been destined for something more. He had followed his father into the building trade and he enjoyed the work, but he never felt it was his true calling. There had always been a nagging voice in his mind, pushing him to change, to find a new job, to challenge himself. He knew this was his opportunity. He was going to embrace it. Aleksy ran to catch up with the long strides of the Ecclesiarch.

"What happens if we cannot find the answers we are looking for in Keterus? What will you do about the Noxvata?"

"I have been pondering that outcome for some time" admitted Srisk. "My faith in the Lords of the Balance is not what it was."

"Why did you follow them at all?" asked Aleksy.

"I wanted to rid the galaxy of the Moretti. I wanted to provide hope to those who had lost it. Things that I failed to do for my home world. They gave me that opportunity and I believe I have made a difference."

"And now you doubt their motives?"

"I have questioned many a mission and there a few that I have not completed to their satisfaction, especially more recently. The Noxvata possess great knowledge; they do not always reveal this to those who perform the menial tasks. Sometimes we are just pixels of a much bigger picture."

"Maybe you, we, should decide for ourselves" suggested Aleksy.

"What do you mean?" replied Srisk.

"You want to make a difference, you want to help those who need it and to give people hope. So what's stopping us from doing just that? Only we decide."

"We are not Gods" said Srisk abruptly.

"No we aren't, but neither are the Noxvata. Who judges them? Who decides whether the decisions they make are just?"

"It is an interesting concept" agreed Srisk. "I will think on it some more as we travel. We have a lot still to organise. Our next endeavour will require meticulous planning. Tell me Alek Black, have you ever given a massage to a female of your species?"

Aleksy almost spat into his visor.

"Um, Kind of. I'm not sure how successful it was though." He felt his cheeks turn red.

"Well it is a start. There is one last thing" said Srisk.

Suddenly the Ecclesiarch stopped. Aleksy almost collided with him. The tall cloaked figure span and grabbed hold of the glass helm on Aleksy's suit.

"Is everything okay?"

Srisk didn't reply, instead the servos on his power suit whirred as he applied pressure to the transparent sphere. Cracks started to appear all across the visor. Aleksy could hear the 'snick' as Srisk's gauntlets kept squeezing.

"What are you doing?" cried Aleksy. He grabbed hold of the Ecclesiarch's arms but he couldn't prize them apart. Suddenly the life giving helm shattered and the oxygen vented into the atmosphere in an instant hiss. Aleksy grabbed at his throat as his body started to gulp and convulse. He fell to his knees, his chest on fire. He felt as if his lungs were going to explode. The decompression wracked his human body and his arms and legs shook violently. The Ecclesiarch stood motionless.

Just as Aleksy thought he would black out he found himself taking short breaths. He panted in quick succession before finally filling his lungs. He frowned as he stood and looked into the glowing orange eyes of the Ecclesiarch.

"I had to be sure" said Srisk.

"Be sure of what?" replied Aleksy still confused as to why he was managing to breathe on an asteroid with no atmosphere.

"Whatever the Baron had invented, he has passed it on to you. I believe it to be a living technology that creates a symbiosis with its host. When your body's survival mechanisms are called upon it automatically triggers. It is why you can understand our language. Probably why you were able to kill so easily and definitely the reason you are breathing now. You will need to understand and master its use."

With that Srisk turned and continued the descent back to the hab blocks.

"Next time just ask" called Aleksy.

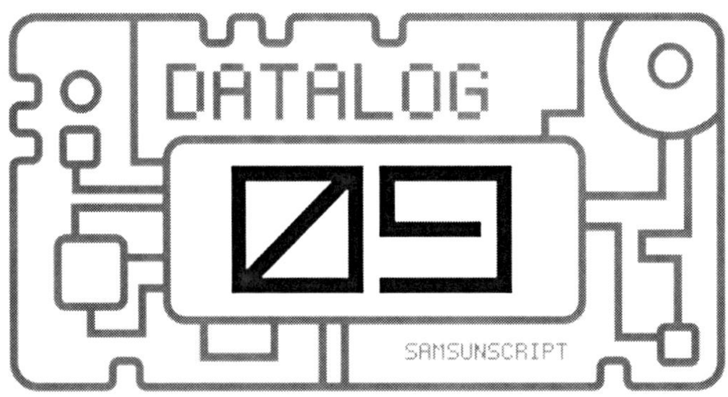

The House of Keterus

Aleksy pulled the long white coat over his body armour and fastened the magnetic toggles down the front. He rolled up the sleeve and tapped on the communication pad.

[What if she doesn't show?]

[She will. She is a creature of precision]

Aleksy looked around the room. It reminded him of a private hospital. Everything was white, bright and clinically clean. The smell of detergent hung in the air. He walked to the single long window that stretched from the floor to the ceiling. He stared out across the wide canal below to where Seelia was waiting on an impressive looking V-foil. She ignored the waving human as the craft bobbed gently in the water.

Keterus Alpha was predominantly a water world. Ninety two percent of its surface was covered by ocean. Its sprawling cities either balanced on gargantuan pillars that allowed it to be raised to cater for the sea state or vast floating atolls that occupied the calmer waters. The latter moved in an undulating unison with the ever changing tides. The capital city of Encorsa was one such entity. It was located high in the Northern hemisphere where the ocean currents faded and the seasonal change in the tides was at its lowest.

The constantly moving city was formed by a series of concentric circles radiating out from a central spire. Each building unit was linked to the next using a pin and pivot system allowing every part of the capital to rise and fall independently. Travel throughout the city was either by air or by using the myriad of canals and waterways that made up its liquid infrastructure.

[Are you ready?] typed Aleksy.

[Yes] came the reply.

[Why don't you wave back then?]

Seelia made a rude gesture with her fingers.

[Very funny] typed Aleksy.

[I'll be ready. Just keep focused on your task. Don't mess this up.]

Aleksy's attention was drawn by voices in the corridor outside. He quickly returned to the semi-circular basin and turned on the tap. He nervously fussed over the pile of towels and could feel his heart rate increasing with every passing moment.

"Now would be a good time to kick in" he said to himself trying to goad the technology that resided within his body to give him a helping hand. To Aleksy's surprise he could suddenly picture a tabular menu in his mind. One of the sections was labelled body modification. He mentally highlighted it. He was overwhelmed by the amount of data it displayed. He moved down through the information and focussed on heart. The image in his mind showed a holographic rendering of the beating organ and a readout alongside indicated one hundred and forty one beats per minute. Next to the display was a virtual dial. Aleksy moved it with his mind and turned the dial to the left. Endorphins flooded his system and his heart rate sank to one hundred and ten.

"Cool!" exclaimed Aleksy not realising that a slender woman had already entered the room.

"What did you say?" she asked.

"Um, nothing my lady" said a flustered Aleksy.

"You will address me as Baroness Rainah. Where is the girl who usually does my massage? I was not informed of a change."

"My apologies Baroness Rainah" Aleksy composed himself. "I was only informed myself earlier this morning. I do not know why."

"Well you're not much good are you?" she scorned. "Show me your hands."

The Baroness grabbed Aleksy's wrists and turned them over. She ran her lithe fingers along his palms.

"They are a bit rough for a masseuse are they not? Where were you trained?"

Aleksy stared at his hands for a moment as his brain sought an answer.

"I trained at the Phoebe Bouffet School of Massage, Baroness Rainah. My hands are a little hard but that's because I specialise in Swedish stone massage" assured Aleksy.

"I've not heard of either. Probably some new age fad no doubt. Anyway let's get on with it. I don't have much time."

"As you wish Baroness Rainah" said Aleksy.

He stared for a moment as the slender figure removed her silky over garment and positioned herself face down on the padded table.

"I assume you are able to open the clasps on my top?" she asked.

Aleksy looked at the four golden clasps that held the back of her tunic together. Even without opening them he could see the flawless skin beneath. He breathed deeply.

"Of course Baroness Rainah. I just need to prepare my oils."

"You should have done that already you stupid boy. Hurry up I don't have all day."

Aleksy turned to the sink and twisted the lever stopping the flow of water. He reached into his pocket and removed the syringe Srisk had given him. He carefully removed the lid that masked the needle and turned towards the prone woman. Unbeknown to Aleksy, the Baroness had an excellent reflected view and saw him approaching. She span quickly and was about to call for her guards. Aleksy panicked and lashed out. He thumped her directly on the eye socket. The Baroness thudded back onto the bed. The blow had knocked her unconscious and a red welt had already appeared around her eye. Aleksy cursed under his breath and looked to the door. It was all quiet. He took the syringe and jabbed it into her shoulder.

"Just for good measure" Aleksy assured himself.

He tapped on his keypad.

[She's out cold.]

[Good. Get the window open and then lower her down] came the reply.

Aleksy walked to the window. Seelia had not moved. He pulled the catch at the base of the glass and pushed it forwards. It moved a short distance and then stopped. Aleksy tried forcing it but the window was only designed to open to allow air in or out. He frantically searched for a release catch, all the while casting a cautious glance back to the still Baroness and the door to the room. His Recit vibrated. It read:

[What's the hold up?]

[Can't open the bloody window] he replied.

[Just get a move on. If I tarry here any longer then the authorities may get suspicious.]

Aleksy grabbed the frame of the window and tried to lift it. To his horror he managed to rip it from its central hinges shattering the glass in the process. A knock sounded on the door.

"Baroness Rainah? Are you okay?"

Aleksy looked around the room for something to wedge against the handle. The only thing tall enough was the massage table. He grabbed the unconscious arm of the Baroness and dragged her onto the floor. He winced as her head slapped against the white tiles.

The locked handle jerked violently as the guards tried to open it. Aleksy rammed the table against the door and applied the brake to the wheels.

He dragged the body of the Baroness to the window. The door was creaking loudly as the guards outside fought to break it down. There was no time to lower the body.

[Get ready to fish her out] tapped Aleksy.

[What!?] Was Seelia's reply, but Aleksy didn't have time to read it. He manhandled the dead weight of the Baroness to the lip of the window and unceremoniously threw her out. He watched as her limp body slapped against the water. Once against he screwed his face up at the sound. Seelia manoeuvred the V-foil alongside the floating body and strained to pull the Baroness from the water.

The door splintered open, and Aleksy jumped. Gunfire echoed around the room and bullets followed his exit to the canal below. Aleksy had not expected to leap as far as he did and instead of coming to land in the water he ripped through the fabric cover on the rear of the V-foil and crashed into the wooden decking. He had landed on his feet. He had fully expected to break every bone in both legs but the advanced technology that filled his every cell cushioned the fall. The deck splintered under the impact but Aleksy stood unharmed. Seelia stared at him.

"Don't ask" said Aleksy.

Seelia nodded to the sodden body in her hands just as bullets peppered the craft. Aleksy slid across and pulled the Baroness from the water with one swift movement.

"Get this thing moving!" he yelled.

Aleksy dragged the body across the deck and into the forward cabin. He could see that her left eye was now completely closed over and black with a bruise. She was also bleeding from several glass cuts. Shaking his head he went to climb the ladder up to the control deck. The engines roared and the quad impellors launched the V-foil forwards. Aleksy shot backwards and landed on top of the soaking body of the Baroness.

"This is like a flaming Carry On movie" he grumbled.

Aleksy's Recit crackled.

"Do you have her?" asked Srisk.

"Yes" replied Aleksy. "Although we might be coming in a little hot." Aleksy instinctively ducked as gunfire strafed the back of the boat.

"What do you mean?" asked the Ecclesiarch.

It was Seelia who typed a response.

[This idiot has managed to attract every guard in the precinct. I am headed to our rendezvous point now but we will have company.]

"Understood" replied Srisk. "Get here as soon as you can. We'll be waiting."

Aleksy clambered into the wheel room just as Seelia span the steering to the right. Again he skidded across the floor and collided with a control panel.

"A bit of notice would be good" shouted Aleksy. He made his way to Seelia's side and gripped the back of a chromed chair firmly. They were speeding down one of the busy canal highways. Seelia was doing her very best to avoid the commuting traffic but with the chasing Royal guard peppering the back of the V-foil she couldn't avoid bouncing off some of the smaller watercraft.

"Wow you can really drive this thing" said Aleksy.

Seelia glared at him. She nodded insistently to the back of the wheelhouse. Aleksy followed her eye-line but he couldn't see anything that merited attention.

"What? What do you want?"

"My gun" she said. "Grab it and start shooting back you imbecile."

"You spoke!" exclaimed Aleksy.

"Can't really take my hands off the wheel to type" she said in a forced calmness.

Aleksy tumbled towards the back of the cabin and grabbed the sniper rifle that was swinging like a pendulum. He stuffed several magazines into the pockets of the white coat he was still wearing and made his way towards the stern.

Smoke was pouring from the back of the damaged V-foil and the once pristine craft was now peppered with bullet holes and the resulting debris. Aleksy dived behind the bulkhead as another salvo ripped across the deck and shattered the small windows next to him. He looked into his mind, to the controls he had accessed earlier. He noticed a label marked [Defence]. On closer examination he read the words [Shield - Auto Enabled] beneath it. Taking a deep breath Aleksy leant around the doorway.

There were two bright orange motor launches in close pursuit. Equally radiant lights rotated and flashed on a long cluster across the roof of each. It was accompanied by a wailing siren that droned in and out of audible frequency. Positioned on the prow of each vessel was a twin barrelled assault cannon with a clear plexi-glass surround. The security officer behind this physical shield squeezed the trigger with practised zeal.

Another salvo pock marked the deck. Splinters shot into the air and the final two rounds hit Aleksy in the thigh and high in the shoulder. He staggered backwards reeling from the impact. He looked down expecting to see blood pouring from the wound but instead the area around the impact zone undulated as his body shield absorbed the bullet. He rubbed his shoulder and apart from the shock of being hit, he was unharmed.

Aleksy raised the long rifle to his shoulder. A reticule blinked into his vision and a request popped into his mind.

[Connect to Quasar EPOG?]

He had no idea what a Quasar EPOG was, but assumed it was the gun.

"Yes" he said out loud.

The crosshair then became emboldened in his eye. Aleksy moved the gun and the reticule followed.

"Awesome" he grinned.

Aleksy walked out across the wreckage of the rear deck and aimed the rifle towards one of the following craft. No sooner had he thought about zooming in on his target, when a supersized image of the Keteran bodyguard filled his right eye. It was a bit confusing having a different view in each eye, so he closed the left one. The cross-hair changed colour as he hovered over the guard's head. Aleksy squeezed the trigger.

Still zoomed, he saw the bullet hit the protective shield and a cobweb of white lines spiral out from the epicentre.

"Dammit!" cursed Aleksy.

He moved the gun barrel and scanned the target. A thin smile crept across his face. He pulled the trigger again. This time the round went under the shield and into the shin of the shocked guard. The sabot round obliterated his leg and the bodyguard fell screaming to the deck.

Aleksy adopted a wide stance to try and steady himself against the violent twisting of the boat. His internal tech provided him with a gyroscopic stability and he found it easy to hold and aim the sniper rifle as the V-Foil bucked beneath him. A blast from the front gunner of the other chasing boat hammered into the side of the V-foil. Aleksy instinctively ducked, but then instantly realised he didn't need to. He straightened his back and then fired. This time the bullet hit the remaining guard in the ankle. The force of the shot ripped the foot clean away. The bodyguard fell backwards just as the boat bounced hard into the wake and the screaming man was flung from the vessel.

Aleksy focused on the cabin. He fired a single shot and then three more. The first round was stopped by the impact resistant glass, as was the second and third, but the fourth high powered slug hit in exactly the same place as all the rest and smashed through the toughened windscreen. Aleksy closed his eyes and coughed as the image of the driver's exploding head filled his vision.

Opening his eyes, he watched as the pilot-less boat veered wildly into the other orange pursuit craft. Aleksy felt the blistering hot wave of the resulting detonation wash over him and his biometric sensors flashed a warning of the temperature increase. He was about to congratulate himself on his achievements when the roar of engines echoed across the canal and the V-foil lurched to the right. Four more security launches emerged from side avenues to join the one that had just rammed into their side. Worse than that the high pitched squeal of jet turbines signalled the arrival of an airborne threat. The hawk-nosed ship had the white markings of the agency and as it banked to the left Aleksy could see the formidable weaponry slung under each stubby wing.

Gunfire erupted from the orange vessel that kept slapping against the side of the V-foil. The close range salvo opened a wide gash across the struggling boat's midsection. Luckily the bullets had passed over the still unconscious baroness. Aleksy was amazed at how little regard they had for her safety. Perhaps they were unaware she was even aboard. Another volley ripped into the rear of the V-foil and one of the engines coughed black smoke.

Seelia shouted over the Recit.

"Do something!"

Aleksy dropped the sniper rifle and vaulted up the rear stairs. He ran to the edge and as the chasing vessel slammed into them once again he jumped. He landed on the other side of the gunner and had to hold on to the chromed rails to stop himself sliding off into the water. Aleksy grabbed hold of the shocked guard with both hands and twisted his body.

He threw the flailing man almost twenty metres. Aleksy grimaced as he saw the body slam into the mirrored glass of a nearby building.

The propellers of the security boat whined as the craft left the water. They had hit a small passenger ferry which had lofted them into the air. Aleksy reached for the handles of the assault cannon and as they landed he inadvertently pulled the trigger. He stumbled to his left and the spray of bullets arced over the V-foil scorching a trail of destruction across the buildings that lined the canal.

Aleksy locked eyes with the helmsman as he tried to turn the gun back on itself. He cursed as the security measures kicked in, stopping its rotation. Without thinking Aleksy heaved upwards and tore the heavy weapon from its moorings. He smiled inside as he saw the angry face of the driver turn to fear. The twin barrels rattled as Aleksy obliterated the wheelhouse and the guard inside. He threw the salvaged gun back across to the V-foil and jumped just as he heard the distinctive whump, whump of launching mortar rounds.

A large plume of water fountained into the air as the projectile exploded under the surface. A moment later the boat that Aleksy had been stood upon erupted upwards breaking in half as it did so.

Recovering the assault cannon Aleksy aimed at the hovering aircraft and opened up. The heavy rounds pummelled the unsuspecting vehicle and a turbine blew out. Fire vented into the air as the stricken craft span out of control and finally crashed into the side of the canal. Cascading explosions started to punch out the glass windows of the buildings above. Aleksy aimed at the remaining boats but the weapon just clicked. Ripping it from its housing had severed the ammunition feed and it was now empty. More and more vessels were joining the chase and in the distance dozens of black specks were filling the air.

Aleksy was about to inform Srisk of the situation when the downdraft of four engines almost halted the V-foil. Aleksy looked up to see the graffiti covered hull of the Desolation hover overhead. Seelia throttled off just as the rear blister turret opened fire. The chug-chug of the cycling barrels reverberated off the buildings as the huge calibre guns annihilated everything behind them.

Aleksy ran below and called to Seelia. She was already on her way out. Aleksy grabbed the body of the Baroness and slung it over his shoulder before returning topside. Seelia was already climbing the wire ladder towards the open door. Ortig waited with his massive stone arm outstretched. He hauled Seelia into the ship and then his head peered back out.

"Catch!" shouted Aleksy.

Grabbing the Baroness by her neck and rump he threw her upwards. He smiled as Ortig's rocky fingers grasped her leg and dragged her inside.

Aleksy bent his legs and jumped. He landed on the lip of the door but started to topple backwards. A firm hand clamped around his forearm and he breathed a sigh of relief as the giant stone warrior helped him inside. Both Seelia and Ortig were staring at him clearly expecting an explanation. Before he could reply Srisk's voice boomed over the Recit.

"Aleksy, did you not understand the plan?"

"I did, but things went a bit wrong."

"A bit?! We have most of Encorsa after us. This was supposed to be a discreet kidnapping.

"Give me a break!" said Aleksy "Until today the only thing I have ever fired in anger was a paintball gun."

"Well come and put those new found skills to the test. Get in the top turret. Seelia I'll need you on the front. Liktus get this rusty lump of metal out of here."

The four turbines rotated as the tug started to power away from the floating city. They were still a long way from safety as the remaining air defence force scrambled after them and the steel ring that drifted in orbit around the planet activated its weapon systems.

Aleksy climbed the tubular ladder and slid into the clear blister that sat between the two tail fins. He secured the four point harness at his chest and quickly moved the seat controls so that he was a comfortable distance from the gun handles.

"Are you plugged in?" asked Srisk over the comms.

"Kind of" replied Aleksy. He had already bonded with the weapon interface as he climbed. Once again a reticule appeared as an overlay on his vision.

"Pull the two levers by your feet and then prime..."

Before Srisk could finish his instructions he saw four lines of tracer ammunition streak out above him. The Ecclesiarch smiled as Aleksy's weapon centred its fire on an ascending box wing fighter.

Most modern defensive shields could repel plasma and other energy based weaponry. However, they struggled when it came to the older projectile ordinance. The huge calibre slugs would cause the shield to ripple. This caused peaks and troughs in the invisible protection. If a bullet hit the thin skin of the trough then it would more than likely rupture and detonate on the ship's hull. Older vessels like the Desolation originally had very crude shielding technology that would only deflect one or two direct hits, after that it relied on its thick Graphene and Modectile plating to protect it. Luckily the old tug had been upgraded with a shield of the more modern variety so it had the best of both worlds. The only downside to so much armour was speed.

The fleet of Keteran craft swarmed after the veteran ship and it was soon the centre of a violent plasma storm. The Desolation was not without teeth and the three turrets span and rotated sending out molten streams of devastating firepower.

Aleksy braced himself in his seat as he rolled upwards tracking another box wing fighter. His adaptive bio-technology gave him exceptionally fast reflexes and the small bursts from his quad-barrels accurately ripped a hole in the looping ship. Once through the shielding the solid rounds didn't have the same destructive power as plasma, but Aleksy quickly learned that and direct hits around the central burner would ignite the fuel cells and the resulting starbursts lit up the sky above the ocean world.

"Yes!" whooped Aleksy. "That's six so far. How many have you got?"

"We do not keep count" replied the Ecclesiarch.

[Four] came the typed response from Seelia.

"Focus on the task at hand" berated Srisk. "Liktus anytime now you can engage the blink drive."

"I am trying Master, but I am still not sure how it works. I do not know if we can even make a jump in this dense atmosphere."

The ship rocked as numerous shots were absorbed.

"We don't have any choice. Activate it now" demanded the Ecclesiarch.

Aleksy held in the twin triggers as a larger star-craft descended from out of the clouds. Small explosions highlighted its underbelly but it was much bigger than the nimble fighters and the outpouring from Aleksy's guns seemed to make little difference. A blue light intensified from a forward battery and suddenly the Desolation shook violently. Alarms sounded and Aleksy could see a red light illuminate in the tube below him.

"The shields are gone. We cannot withstand another hit. Liktus how is it going?" Srisk's question hung in the air. Aleksy watched the bright blue ball grow once again as the attacking ship charged its primary weapon. It reached critical mass but then froze. The bullet trail from his glowing barrels slowed and the spinning fighters followed suit. Time stopped. The next moment the blackness of space surrounded them and all was quiet and still.

*

Srisk administered an antidote to the Baroness. She stirred and opened one eye.

"Forgive the bonds" said Srisk. "But I have learnt my lesson when dealing with your kind."

The Baroness lifted her cuffed wrists and touched a slender finger to her eye.

"Ah yes. You'll have to forgive that also. He is very new to all of this."

Srisk turned to look at Aleksy. Rainah quickly recovered her composure and within moments she had read and digested the situation.

"You are one of the Noxvata's lackeys are you not? Don't tell me they are behind this? I am holding up my end of the bargain. Explain yourself" demanded the Baroness.

Srisk grabbed the front of his hood and pulled it further forward.

"I do not speak for the Lords of the Balance."

"Then what is the meaning of this intrusion? I am a Baroness of the Royal Household. Do you know what will happen to you and your crew of freaks when this gets out?"

"I am past caring about the multitude of possible eventualities Baroness. I am now only concerned with the mechanisms that I can control. I am after the truth."

"You are speaking in riddles. What is it you want?" hissed Rainah.

Srisk leant closer to his captive.

"I have cut the leash that held me in check. I now operate of my own free will. I want answers. I will get them from you if I have to cut every limb from your body or scramble every cell in your brain. Is that clear enough for you Baroness Rainah."

For the first time the polished visage of the Baroness slipped and Aleksy could see fear in her eyes.

"The Noxvata. Explain to me your agreement with them."

Rainah shifted uncomfortably in her chair.

"My brother Valah is, annoyingly, a genius. He has developed a type of folding technology that can be deployed aboard any starship. It will allow a fleet to jump in and out of any point in space. In his infinite wisdom my brother decided he did not agree with the Household's plan on how this technology should be utilised, and promptly disappeared. My agreement with the Lords of the Balance was simple, they would find my brother and deliver him and his technology to me."

"What did they ask for in return?" enquired Aleksy.

"You!. You are the masseuse? I have already told you how to address me correctly have I not?"

"You have" said Aleksy "I have chosen to ignore it and because you're the one tied up in a chair, I think you should just answer the question."

"Insolence!" muttered the Baroness.

"Answer the question" demanded Srisk.

Rainah sighed.

"In return I agreed that the combined Houses of Keterus would provide an armada."

"For what purpose?"

The Baroness looked confused.

"How little you know about the universe" she goaded.

"Then enlighten me" said Srisk calmly.

"To take back dark space. What else? To drive the filthy Moretti from our galaxy once and for all. Don't tell me that doesn't make your skin tingle."

"The Federation would veto any direct action. They would not dare break the peace."

"No, you are correct. They would not. That is why my agreement with the Lords of the Balance did not involve the senile leaders of the Federation. They would fester in indecision for another century if we let them. We needed to act first before the Moretti decided for themselves that they have had enough of this pallid truce."

"I would see the Moretti driven back to the hole they sprang from but even with your armada you could not stop the tide of aggression that would pour forth."

"Indeed we could not" agreed the Baroness. "That is why we needed the folding technology. The fleet will sail to Mai'Len and destroy as many worlds as it can. Before the Moretti horde can mobilise we will jump back behind the safety of the Defensive Necklace. They will no doubt retaliate and in so doing will force the hand of the Federation. They will have no choice."

"You seek a return to all out war?"

"You make it sound like a bad thing. Mai'Len is but our first objective. With the might of the entire Federation behind us we can jump in and obliterate world after world. We will push them back through the Wolf Gate."

Seelia looked at Srisk and typed on her console.

[Don't we want the same thing?]

"We do" nodded Srisk. "But something does not sit right. He turned back to the Baroness.

"How long until your fleet is assembled?"

Rainah tilted her head back and laughed.

"Assembled? Oh my dear Ecclesiarch how naive you really are. The armada is already en route from the Gee Eight Gate. More than five thousand vessels will be descending upon Mai'Len within the week. It is probably the reason why you managed to escape my home world so easily, as we left it virtually unguarded. Did you think my abduction would stop our advance? You really are a fool."

"How did you get hold of the folding technology?" asked Srisk.

"Do you think you and your team are the only Warriors of the Balance? The Noxvata delivered it to us over six months ago. Our ships are already equipped. War is inevitable I'm afraid."

Srisk turned to the crew.

"Something is not right. The Noxvata seek the balance of all things. This move would see the Federation tip the scales in their favour. I have my doubts about the Noxvata's intent and indeed my encounter with the Moretti Guardian goes unexplained, but I have never known them reveal a hand so one sided before. I am concerned that we are missing a piece of this puzzle."

Seelia tapped away on her comms unit.

[The Baron wouldn't hand over that technology? And how did they find him? It took us two years to get close to him. There's no way they could have stolen it without Valah finding out. Perhaps she is bluffing.]

"Perhaps" replied Srisk.

"I agree with Seelia" added Aleksy. "The Baron died before he would give up his secrets."

The Ecclesiarch and Seelia both rounded on the human.

"My brother is dead?" stuttered Rainah.

"Oops" whispered Aleksy.

"Well?" insisted the Baroness. "At least do me the courtesy."

"Yes" admitted Srisk. "Valah is dead."

The Baroness lowered her head.

"Look" started Aleksy. "We keep getting all these bits of information and we are still not sure what's happening. I think we need to talk to the organ grinder and stop wasting time with the monkeys."

[What are you talking about?] typed Seelia.

"We need to speak to those who call the shots, pull the strings, you know the ones in charge" Aleksy held up his hands. "The Lord of the Balance!" he exclaimed.

Srisk inhaled. His breathing filter burbled with the low treble of his breath.

"I hate to admit it, but the Terran is correct. Sangelon will hold the answers. Liktus, jump us into the Ninth Cloud."

FOUR - Warriors of the Balance -Samsun Lobe

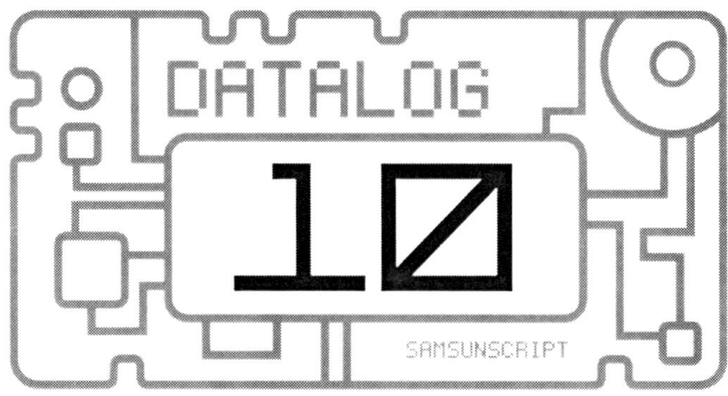

The Faceless

Aleksy squeezed the contents from the tube into his ceramic pan. He had expected it to suddenly pop into a delicious looking meal. Instead, the beige sludge resembled a melting sandworm. Aleksy poked it with his spork. He turned the tube over in his hand and re-read the label.

[Meat Protein - Pro-digestic]

It even sounded disgusting.

The door to the galley slooshed open and the silver skinned Seelia sidled in. She took a metallic packet and placed it inside the moleculiser. Aleksy typed on his forearm console with his forefinger.

[What are you having? I have managed to find a portion of cat vomit]

Seelia turned a dial, and the machine whirred into life.

"What is a cat?"

"You're speaking again! I thought I'd dreamt it back on Keterus."

"I've watched your one finger typing. It's painful. It would take a light-year to hold a conversation with you."

Aleksy chuckled.

"Yea that's true. Me and technology have never been that close. Ironic."

"So" Seelia sat opposite. Aleksy looked at his foetid food substitute.

"Umm it's meat protein or something" he explained.

"No you fool. What is a cat?"

Aleksy blushed and laughed nervously.

"They are a sort of small furry, four legged animal. We keep them as pets. My mate's Gran has six of them."

"Sounds revolting."

"What about your world? Do you have pets?"

"My world is sterile. Any non-purposeful organism would be eradicated."

"Sounds like a bleak place."

"It is."

"Is that why you don't speak?" probed Aleksy.

"I chose not to speak as there was nobody worth speaking with. I have grown up in an environment where everybody communicates using a device. I know you find that strange but it is normal for me. Verbal connection is... strange."

"You'd get on well with my little sister. She is permanently attached to her phone, although she does also talk. A lot."

"Tell me Alek."

She said his name slowly. Aleksy liked how it sounded.

"How were you able to do what you did, back there on Keterus? Are you and Srisk keeping something from me?"

"No" Aleksy said quickly. "It's nothing like that. I have only just discovered how to use it. Srisk thinks that somehow the Baron transferred it to me before he died. Perhaps he thought I was from Keterus. I still am not sure how it works. I sort of see things in my mind. I call it 'dream-tech'. I still have no clue as to what it can do."

"Let's try something" suggested Seelia.

Aleksy's cheeks turned crimson for a second time. 'There must be a control to stop me blushing' he thought. Seelia slid her hands across the table and her slender silver fingers grasped Aleksy's wrist. Her touch was ice cold, like her digits were actually made from silver.

"What do you want me to do?" he asked.

"Just sit there and relax" replied Seelia.

Aleksy closed his eyes and immediately thought of cats. He tried to relax which was proving difficult as his heart was racing. He heard an echo. He concentrated on the sound and then suddenly it became clear.

<Can you hear me?>

"Yes, of course I can" said Aleksy confused.

<I am not talking out loud. I have reached out to your mind.>

"What!? Like Telepathy?"

<Sort of. Now try answering with your thoughts rather than your vocal chords>

Aleksy screwed up his face in concentration. He focused on his bio-menu but there wasn't anything that made sense under the communications tab.

<I don't know what to do> he thought.

<That's it!> exclaimed Seelia.

<You can hear me? I am just talking inside my head>

<Yes I can hear you, but try not to be so loud>

<Sorry> replied Aleksy still unintentionally shouting.

Aleksy opened his eyes as he felt Seelia release her grip and the sound of her chair scrape across the metal floor.

"Is that it?" he asked.

Seelia paused.

"If we're going to be working together it may prove useful to be able to link minds. Your species have yet to utilise the more interesting parts of your brains but I concluded that the Baron's addition to your limbic system could create the connections you required. It's very interesting."

"Does this mean we won't speak again?" Aleksy asked.

"Maybe we will" smiled Seelia.

She walked to the door. Aleksy wanted to call after her but neither words spoken or unspoken came out. As the door slid shut Aleksy pushed the unappetising meal across the table.

*

After Srisk's voiceprint had been verified by a surprised operator, the cumbersome and bulky tug was granted access to the gargantuan rolling metropolis of Obscura. There had been heated debate amongst the team as to who should enter the city to confront the Noxvata. Srisk had wanted to go alone but Aleksy and Seelia were keen to accompany him. Ortig had quickly agreed to stay with the ship and guard the Baroness.

The rear landing gantry lowered and Srisk, Seelia and Aleksy walked down the ramp. The small red figure of Liktus stood forlorn at the top. The Ecclesiarch turned.

"I know. I know. Stay with the ship" he sighed.

"Not this time my friend. I will need your expertise. Bring your console."

Liktus jumped up and down with excitement.

"Now" added Srisk.

"Yes Master" beamed the crimson reptile.

Two mechanical servitors escorted the party into the city and towards the inner sanctum. The corridors were as devoid of life as they normally were. The footsteps of the Ecclesiarch's power suit echoed through the warren of hallways.

"Where is everyone?" asked Aleksy.

"There is little to no sentient life in Obscura, at least that I am aware of, apart from those that visit obviously. The city is entirely automated. The only things you will encounter are servitors, like these, droids or sentry mechanoids."

"Then the Noxvata won't be here either?"

"That would be logical" answered Srisk.

Aleksy looked at the others searching for some back up, urging them to ask the obvious question. They didn't, so he did.

"Then what are we doing in this ghost city?"

"Following the thread" said Srisk.

Aleksy looked down at Liktus. The wide glassy eyes stared back at him.

"He likes to be dramatic" whispered Liktus.

"I can hear you" grunted Srisk.

As they reached the imposing doors to the inner sanctum, Aleksy's jaw dropped in awe of the intricate carvings that covered the gateway. As they started to open, one of the Servitors blocked the way forward.

"Just yourself Ecclesiarch, beyond this point. I must request that you leave your weapons here also." The Servitor's voice was metronomic. The robotic servant held out three metal digits.

"Of course" replied Srisk.

He flicked his long cloak away and took his mag-locked whisper rifle from his back, carefully placing on the machine's outstretched arms. As his fingers curled around the hilt of his molecular sword it hummed with power and a swift chop saw the Servitor's head bounce along the corridor. At the same time Seelia had drawn her side arm and from point blank range shot a hole in the temple of the other robot. Aleksy flinched as electronic and metal debris vented from the smouldering hole in its head.

"We won't have long before the security protocol is invoked" explained Srisk. "When that happens you'll have less than three minutes to get back to the ship."

As they walked into the sanctum Aleksy could not help but stare at the walls and ceilings. He had visited Salisbury Cathedral and had seen a few documentaries on the Sagrada Familia in Barcelona but this was unlike anything he could have imagined. The detail, realism and craftsmanship that had gone into the construction of the sanctum was unparalleled.

Not concentrating on where he was going Aleksy bumped into the back of the Ecclesiarch.

"Sorry" he whispered.

In front of them stood the five monoliths that Srisk had described. They were all blank. A ghost image flickered across the central pillar and then a white shadowy face appeared.

"This is not a scheduled meeting Ecclesiarch, and who are the others with you? This is a direct breach of the code."

There was a moment's silence as the remaining four spectral images appeared on the other obsidian slabs.

"Explain yourself Ecclesiarch" demanded the central stone.

"I am here to report. You gave a me a mission or have your forgotten?"

The second stone from the right glowed.

"Remember to whom you address Ecclesiarch. I can feel the tension within you but you should not lose your decorum."

"My apologies" bowed Srisk. He looked behind the black monoliths to where Liktus sat with his console plugged into the rear of one of the stones. The small creature shook his head. Srisk continued. "This is Seelia, the assassin you directed me to recruit." Seelia bowed. "This is Alek Black, I saw fit to bring him onto my team after the loss of Centurio Agorius." Aleksy stepped forward and bowed.

"It's nice to meet everybody" Aleksy said in his most polite voice.

"He still has much to learn" added Srisk.

Again there was a moment's silence.

"Report."

"It has taken us longer than expected to track down Baron Valah, but I assume you are well aware of the very good reason for that. Sadly I must report that we, or rather I have failed in my overall mission once again. After locating the Baron, we pursued him but he tragically died in the encounter. His body was destroyed."

"And the folding technology?" asked one of the Lords.

"That remained with the Baron's ship, The Dawn of Light. We inflicted severe damage but it trans-located before we had a chance to board. I assume you no longer need it. I have been made aware that you already possess the technology required for blink travel."

This time the silence was much longer.

"Indeed we do" came the reply.

The central stone lit up.

"Tell me Ecclesiarch did you really think we would not be able to see through your deceit. As a master of lies it is easy for me to uncover those who only dabble in the skill. Your reprehension is long overdue. I have to say I am disappointed."

Liktus peered from behind the stone slabs and gave a thumbs up signal. Srisk straightened.

"There was a time when those words would have stung, but I have followed your lies for long enough. This time I am here for answers."

Suddenly a loud klaxon sounded and all but the central monolith shut down and started to descend into the sanctum floor. The remaining slab glowed.

"I am not sure what you have planned Ecclesiarch, but the security protocol has been activated. Good luck making your escape."

The stone went black and started to sink.

"Well Liktus what did you find?"

The small creature was still pulling leads from the back of the lowering stone.

"As we suspected Master they are all off world except one. I am sending the location to your system."

"What now?" asked Aleksy.

"It is time for you to get back to the ship. The next part I must do alone."

"You will need our help" said Aleksy.

"If you are still inside the city when the security countdown reaches zero you will be of no help to me. Get going now. Do not stop. If you do not hear from me within twenty minutes then you must leave."

"Master" Liktus looked up sadly. The Ecclesiarch's knee joints whirred as he knelt to face the red creature.

"Thank you for your help Liktus. Look after the others for me."

*

The blurting sound of the warning klaxon rang in their ears as they ran through the long black walled corridors. Liktus clung to Seelia's shoulders as they hurried towards the spaceport. They crossed an intersection and white hot plasma bolts scorched the dark walls around them. Two sentry mechanoids closed from the adjoining passageways, their rotating cannons automatically targeting the movement ahead of them.

Liktus jumped to the ground and hurried towards the control panel. He plugged in his console and tapped furiously on the keyboard. Seelia and Aleksy ducked around the end of the wall only to be pinned back by deadly accurate fire. Seelia dived into the intersection and fired a swift volley of shots before rolling to safety in the opposite corridor.

"They're shielded" she called out. "Cover me, I'm coming back."

Aleksy rounded the corner and squeezed the trigger of the stubby mauler. Srisk had given him the assault weapon before they had disembarked. It had a snub barrel with six chambers that rotated as it fired. The hollow rounds were filled with korium. Once the slug had punched into the body of its victim the radioactive substance inside the bullet spread like confetti tearing the organs apart. It was very effective on bio-organisms but had little effect against a shielded droid.

White circles spread across the sentry's shield as Aleksy kept the trigger held in. A bolt of energy suddenly slammed into his shoulder and sent him face first into the wall. Aleksy slid down onto the hexagonal flooring, blood pouring from his nose. Seelia slid in next to him and pulled him to safety as another barrage of plasma obliterated the corner of the corridor.

"That's it" shouted Liktus. "Quickly, get inside."

The blast doors thumped shut. Seelia moved Liktus to one side and fired a single bolt into the control panel. A solitary point on the top of the sealed door started to glow.

"They're cutting through" said Liktus.

Aleksy wiped the blood from his face and picked up the small red creature.

"Come on, we have to keep moving."

They crossed another two intersections and then came to another security gate. Liktus tapped Aleksy on the shoulder.

"Just around the corner is the outer door to the landing pads. If we close this one it will give us more time."

Aleksy nodded and helped Liktus to the ground. He turned to Seelia.

"How do we stop those things?"

"The shields won't last forever. Sustained fire will weaken them and eventually a shot will get through, or else we have to get really close to them and switch them off."

"We'll be dead by then" declared Aleksy not seeing the humour in her comments.

Seelia ignored him.

"How are your injuries?"

Aleksy touched his finger to the tip of his nose.

"It's not serious. My shield or whatever it is protected me from the initial blast, although I don't think I will be able to take many more of those."

More shots rang out overhead and they had time to see several more sentry mechanoids accelerate towards them before Liktus closed the blast door.

"Just one more door to go" smiled Liktus.

"Then what?" asked Aleksy. "Won't they have guns out on the landing pads? How will we get to the ship?"

"One problem at a time" suggested Seelia.

Aleksy rounded the corner and then instantly started to back pedal as a flurry of plasma bolts hammered into the end of the corridor.

"We have a bigger problem" panted Aleksy. "There's another one of those tracked killer robot things blocking the way to the landing pads."

Several points on the door behind them started to glow and a small blue flame appeared as the sentries on the other side attempted to cut their way in. Aleksy crouched down and placed his hands on his head.

"This is no time for despair" chided Seelia.

"I'm thinking" snapped Aleksy.

Seelia smiled to herself.

"I wondered what the noise was."

Aleksy didn't hear her. He was scrolling through the maze of options in his mind. He stumbled across a 'blink travel' dialogue box but dismissed it. He focussed on biometrics and then selected the speed entry. He mentally moved the scrubber to maximum. Aleksy stood. He waved his hands in front of his face. They shifted in a blur like a ghost image followed each movement.

"Cool" said Aleksy.

"What's happening to you?" asked Seelia.

"I'm about to find out. Give me some cover, but don't hit me."

Before Seelia could ask another question Aleksy rounded the corner and drew the long combat knife strapped to his lower back. He sprinted towards the sentry. The bolts of plasma erupted from both arm units of the mechanoid but they appeared in slow motion. Aleksy ran towards the side of the corridor and to his amazement his amplified speed carried him up the wall. He thought back to his youth when he had played with his hot wheels cars and how if they were going fast enough they could loop the loop. Aleksy ran across to the other side avoiding the constant stream of molten death that was being pumped out from the twin cannons of the sentry. His immense speed took him up the wall and along the roof and over the head of the droid.

Aleksy dropped onto its shoulders and stabbed the long serrated blade straight through the top of its domed head. Sparks fizzed and the mechanoid lurched to one side. Aleksy grabbed the chin of the sparking head and pulled. His enhanced strength tore it away. Even without its main sensor array the security droid continued to fire. Aleksy reached inside its chest and randomly grabbing handfuls of cable pulled out its electronic innards. The left arm cannon died but the right spasmed and started to blast holes in the ceiling.

Aleksy swung down and using his body weight turned the pulsing cannon inwards. The blasts blew its left track to pieces before a final shot to its lower stanchion silenced the killing machine.

Seelia and Liktus ran towards him. The silver skinned woman reached out with her mind.

< I'm impressed >

Before Aleksy could muster the attention to reply the security protocol countdown hit zero. A high pitched sound reverberated throughout the city. The destructive frequency brought all livings things to their knees. Aleksy screamed and cupped his hands to his ears as the acute pitch hammered into his mind. Seelia and Liktus writhed in agony as the constant sound battered their senses.

*

Srisk looked at the data Liktus had sent him. They had gambled that they would be able to trace the signals that the Noxvata were channelling via the black monoliths. They hadn't expected any of them to be close, but it would have given them a place to start looking. As expected four of the five signals were off world but surprisingly one was being emitted from Sangelon, within the confines of Sangelon itself. Liktus had pinpointed the location deep within the bowels of the creeping city. Srisk surveyed the schematic and decided the direct approach would be the most efficient.

The Ecclesiarch reached up and smashed the camera inset above the elevator doors. It wouldn't keep him hidden for long but he hoped it would mask his location for the next thirty seconds at least. Srisk placed the explosive ordinance on the elevator floor ensuring it faced the doors. The lift closed and he pressed the button marked 'sub-floor eleven'. As the motors whined the Ecclesiarch pried his metal fingertips between the doors and then his suit moaned as he levered them apart.

He looked down into the regularly lit shaft. As the elevator car stopped and the doors to sub floor eleven opened he activated the remote detonator. Flames and hot vapour shot up between the gaps around the close fitting unit but the full focused force of the explosion emptied outwards. The remnants of the elevator crashed against the sides and the fragmented pieces clattered down into the blackness. Srisk could feel the rush of oxygen as the fire below sucked in its vital fuel. He reached out to the dangling metal rope that hung in the lift shaft and plummeted towards the chaos.

Sparks streamed from his gauntlet as he squeezed the cable, slowing his descent. Srisk released his grip and jumped to the charred hallway. The city's fire suppressant system was already in full flow and cream foam covered the wreckage. Around the edges it had started to harden into a crust. Srisk kicked the disjointed arm of a sentry mechanoid. It skittled across the floor and thudded into the foaming liquid that pumped from the wall vents.

Srisk checked his map. The location was only a short distance away. He was about to move when he heard the familiar clicking noise of an activating weapon. Srisk dived to the side as plasma bolts hammered into the blackened lift shaft. One of the sentries had survived the blast. Srisk reacted instinctively and in one fluid motion he removed the whisper rifle from his back and pumped the under-slung barrel three times. As the explosive rounds detonated against the mechanoid's shield, Srisk pulled the trigger releasing several magnetic slugs from the hand-held rail gun.

He heard the satisfying fizz of ruptured electronics and as he strode confidently through the smoke he placed another two well aimed shots into the heart of the dying machine.

His head-up display flashed as the counter he had set reached zero. The Ecclesiarch shut down his tympanic implants as the high pitched screech filled the city.

Srisk followed the map schematic until he reached an unmarked security hatch. As he looked for the control pad the doors slid open and an archaic voice beckoned him to enter.

The room was circular. There was a small landing where Srisk had entered and steps wound down on either side. It was not what the Ecclesiarch was expecting. The entire space was full of antiques and curiosities. Paper books were stacked precariously, weapons, statues, old power armour and countless unknown objects occupied every nook. It was a horde of treasures from twenty thousand years of history. At the far side of the room was a large throne. Wires and tubes hung from the ceiling and connected to the regal chair. A semi-circular array of monitors surrounded the occupant. He was smaller than Srisk had imagined, slightly smaller even than Aleksy. Although by the look of his aging features that could have been partly due to atrophy. His pallid skin was covered in dark blemishes and the areas of his body not covered with life-preserving technology were almost translucent. His eyes were darker than midnight and Srisk felt drawn towards them like two black holes sucking him in.

The Ecclesiarch walked carefully through the minefield of antiquities towards the throne. Transparent eyelids opened and closed over the glassy eyes and Srisk felt the trance subside.

"Welcome Ecclesiarch. I have often wondered when this day would come to pass." His voice was mainly mechanic, enhanced by the auric implants that poked out from his trachea. The ancient humanoid's lips hardly moved as his speech rasped the air. "We have spoken many times but we have never been formally introduced. I am Sekmhet. It is good to finally meet you in the flesh. Well, what both of us have left that can be defined as flesh that is."

Srisk lifted the whisper rifle to his shoulder and pointed it towards the old Lord.

"There is no need for that Ecclesiarch. There is nothing you can threaten me with that I have not already heard before. I have lived for an eternity and I would welcome death. However you would not have the answers to your questions if you killed me so quickly." The aging Lord moved slowly in his seat and he gestured with his hand. "My apologies I have not cleaned, but you are my first breathing guest in over three hundred years. Please Ecclesiarch, take a seat."

"I would prefer to stand" said Srisk.

"As you wish" smiled the old man. "It is fitting that it was your defiance that first brought you to my radar. All those moons ago. You were so eager to please back then and now look at you. You have lost your faith. It is to be expected."

"You have no idea of what I have lost" retorted Srisk.

"On the contrary young Ecclesiarch I know everything about you, but that is not why you are here. You seek answers. Ask what you will."

"The Keteran fleet sails to Mai'Len. You have given them the folding technology. They will start another war with the Moretti. Why?"

"How little you understand of the universe Ecclesiarch."

"Stop playing games old man and explain yourself" growled Srisk.

"The Houses of Keterus will bring peace to the galaxy not war. Everything is not always as it first seems, but then you should know that Ecclesiarch. We do not have the folding technology to give. That was your mission. If the Baron is truly dead as you say then that has been lost to us."

"But the Baroness. She believes they have it. How can that be?"

"Because we told her so. She craves power so intensely she would be blinded by the truth. We delivered what we promised to her. We told the Baroness that the blink drives would be restricted to a single operation only to prevent any unsanctioned exploitation. We promised we would give her and her people free access to the technology once the mission to Mai'Len was successfully completed. In her haste for war I doubt she would have prepared a test run. If she did the Baroness would find the blink drives are nothing but useless ballast."

"None of them work?"

"As I said. We do not have the technology to give" explained Sekmhet.

"So you will allow an entire nation to venture on a fool's errand. Millions will die."

"No Ecclesiarch. They will all die. The Moretti are patiently waiting for the armada to arrive. We have seen to it."

"You work with the enemy?" Srisk could not believe what he was hearing.

"We work with all sides" said Sekmhet.

"But the Moretti. How can you..."

The aging Lord held up his hand.

"Do not jump to conclusions Ecclesiarch. The mechanisms we employ have taken hundreds of years. Do not expect to understand everything in a heartbeat."

"Then do your very best to explain it to me" insisted Srisk.

"As you may or may not know the Moretti still mourn the passing of their Paragon. A new one will be chosen shortly. When that happens war would have returned to our galaxy if we had not intervened. We have tried on more than one occasion to negotiate with the Moretti. You will know firsthand how difficult that is."

"Kalleeka" said Srisk.

"Exactly. You met the Guardian Murac' Amor. We had identified him as one such candidate we could deal with. Unfortunately he refused our plans. He demanded access to the Federation Gates instead."

"He called it the key"

"Yes he considered it the key to destroying the Federation. Obviously we could not have that. That's why we sent you. We knew you would kill him or at least die trying. Either way our bargain with Murac' Amor was at an end."

"So how does the Keteran armada figure in all of this?"

"We have found a new ally. His name is Goshen' Foran. He is in the front running to become the next Paragon of the Moretti. His overwhelming victory at Mai'Len will seal that eventuality. With Goshen as the new Paragon he will honour his side of the bargain and the Moretti will not seek to extend their territory within the Shakari galaxy. The peace we have enjoyed for the last two hundred years will continue."

"And you believe the Moretti to have honour?" Srisk was disgusted at the thought.

"Only time can answer that question, but rest assured other machinations are in place if Goshen reneges on our agreement."

"What about the millions of innocents that will die. It will practically wipe out the Keteran race; they will never recover from such a loss."

"No one is innocent Ecclesiarch. It is a sacrifice that is made to protect the lives of trillions. It is simple economics. Other races in this galaxy have died out. It is no different."

"I'm sure those who are sailing into your trap would think of it differently."

"Do not lose sleep over the Keterans Ecclesiarch. Ask yourself why they sail? They hunger for power. They would dominate the Federation if they could. These are all things you will come to understand Ecclesiarch. Now that you are here, that you have finally thrown off your bindings, you can fulfil your destiny."

"What are you talking about?" snarled Srisk.

"You did not think you would be leaving this place did you? You have your answers now. You know of our hand in this matter and whether you agree with it or not it will unfold as we have planned. Do not fight the inevitable Ecclesiarch."

The old Lord removed a golden pendant from around his neck. The jewel sparkled with five various coloured stones. He held it out to the Ecclesiarch.

"This is yours now. It is the seal of the Noxvata. It was given to me by my predecessor and now I gift it to you. It is time to remove the cloak of an Ecclesiarch and take your rightful place as one of the Lords of the Balance. You will now decide the fate of the Shakari galaxy."

Srisk stared at the golden necklace. His modified orange eyes glowed as he lifted his head.

"I want nothing more from you. I am tired of the lies and deception. I will change this galaxy by removing each and every one of you foul Lords."

"Look to the screen Ecclesiarch" directed Sekmhet.

As Srisk viewed the flickering display he could see Aleksy, Seelia and Liktus squirming in pain, smearing their own blood across the floor.

"You will stay. You will give me your word as the last Ventorian, that you will stay. Only then will I free your friends. It is your choice Ecclesiarch. Will you allow three more innocents to die on your behalf?"

*

Aleksy retreated inside his mind looking for shelter from the penetrating noise that assaulted his senses. He desperately searched the dataflow for an end to the pain. He managed to close off his hearing and the pain dulled. His head still pounded as he tried to lift himself from the floor. Blood had poured from his ears, eyes and nose and a quick glance to his side saw that Seelia and Liktus were suffering the same. Aleksy opened a Recit channel to the Desolation.

"Ortig. Come in. Are you there?"

"Yes Alek. What is going on?"

"We need your help."

Aleksy looked up to the hangar bay door.

"Door Seven. We need it open."

"What about the Baroness? Srisk said not to leave."

"If you don't we'll be dead within minutes."

The Recit channel went quiet.

Aleksy flopped back to the floor. He crawled across to Seelia and then reached out to drag Liktus close. He lay with his back to the landing bay door trying to protect them both. It was then that he saw a section of the blast door back down the corridor clatter to the ground and the groping arm of a sentry droid forced its way through.

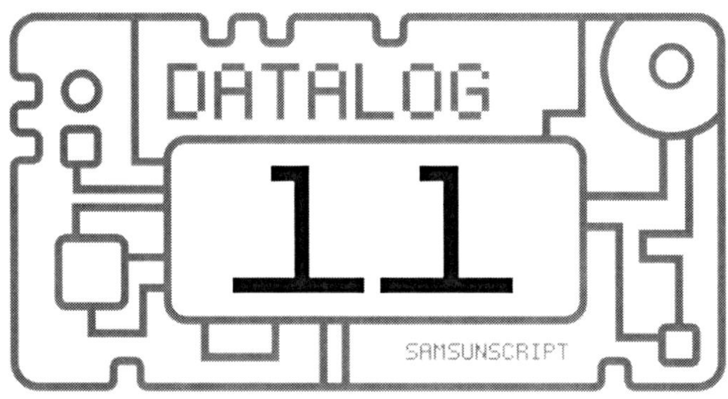

Sky-fall

Aleksy reached for his gun. His bloody fingers curled around the pistol grip. He used Seelia's shoulder as a rest and started to fire at the robotic appendage that was trying to tear through the blast door.

Suddenly a gust of sulphuric air washed over him. He rolled to see the massive forearms of Ortig pulling the gateway apart. The stone skinned giant forced his way through the opening and stooped to cradle his three injured comrades. Lifting them effortlessly from the floor he ran back towards the ramp of the Desolation. White bolts sailed overhead and continued to bombard the senescent tug as the loading door closed.

As soon as they were away from the confines of the city the disabling sound faded. They were all disorientated but Aleksy was recovering quickly.

"Liktus are you okay?"

The small red creature nodded slowly.

"I need you to get the shields up and activate the turrets."

As Liktus limped towards the cockpit, Aleksy knelt beside the wounded woman. He carefully moved her hair from her face. Blood had congealed around her eyes and nose. It reminded him of a stigmata picture he had once seen.

"Can you walk?" Aleksy asked.

"Thank you" said Seelia.

"Don't thank me. It was Ortig that dragged us clear."

"You know what I mean"

"Um Alek" mumbled Ortig.

The Recit crackled.

"Hang on a second Ortig. What is it Liktus?"

"Alek. We have shields but we are taking considerable fire. The city's space-port auto-cannons have come online."

"Great work Liktus. Seelia it's time for some payback."

"Um Alek" repeated Ortig.

"What is it my friend?" replied Aleksy

"The Baroness. She is gone."

"Good. I never liked her anyway. We'll worry about that later, we need to man the guns."

Aleksy helped Seelia towards the gun positions and watched as she slid down the rungs and into the seat. He climbed the ascending ladder quickly and strapped himself into the blister turret. His bio-mechanics were already connected. As soon as his fingers hit the twin triggers Aleksy started targeting the city's defences. The satisfying chug-chug of the archaic guns made Aleksy chuckle as they tore massive holes in the black walls of Obscura.

As Aleksy revelled in the destruction he was causing he felt a tickling sensation in his brain. He knew what it was and a bigger smile beamed across his face as he acknowledged Seelia's mind link.

< How long do we wait? >

< We stay here until Srisk returns >

< What if he doesn't? >

< Then we'll run out of ammo, and at least you won't have to tell him how we managed to let the Baroness escape >

*

Srisk stared at the necklace. He reached out and took it from Sekmhet.

"I stood where you once are. I had my doubts also, but I know I have made a difference. Become all that you can be. Take on the mantle, Lord Srisk."

The Ecclesiarch glanced up at the monitor. He saw Aleksy move across the floor. It was the only sign he needed. Srisk pulled the trigger of the whisper rifle and a solid slug punched a hole as large as his fist in the face of Sekmhet. His life giving monitors complained with a monotonous tone as their ancient host died.

"I will change this galaxy in my own way" declared Srisk.

*

After the Ecclesiarch had explained his encounter with the late Lord Sekmhet and filled them in on the treachery that was about to unfold in Dark Space, he offered them all a choice.

Srisk had decided to warn the Keteran armada of the impending Moretti trap, believing that wholesale slaughter on that scale was not an ethical way to achieve peace. He gave the crew the option of joining him or they could leave and pursue their own futures.

The thought of returning home to be reunited with his family and friends was a strong draw for Aleksy, but part of him wondered what they might say about his absence and about Ralph's death. Besides he was on the adventure of a lifetime and if he was honest with himself there was another reason he wanted to stay.

Seelia had instantly thrown her lot in with the Ecclesiarch. She confessed to having nowhere else to go and being a wanted felon she would have found it difficult to locate a surrogate home.

Liktus had no intention of leaving the Ecclesiarch's side. His reasons and hopes for the future were his own. It was only Ortig that was struggling over the decision, and that was because he didn't understand the question.

"Why can't I stay with you?" he asked.

"You can my friend" explained Srisk. "I am not sending you away. I am giving you the choice to leave if you want to. I would welcome your company, but I cannot take advantage of you anymore. If there is anywhere else you would rather be then I will arrange it."

"What do you mean, take advantage? asked Ortig scratching his stony scalp.

"What do you remember before we met?" replied Srisk.

"Nothing" admitted Ortig.

"Do you remember everything since?"

"Not everything. There are blank bits."

"Yes there are" said Srisk. "The collar you wear. I told you that it protects you. Well that is only partly true. It protects all of us from you also. The collar soothes your mind. When it is switched off rage fills your every cell. You recognise no-one and your fury manifests itself in a indiscriminate killing frenzy. Those are the pieces you cannot remember."

Ortig slowly digested the Ecclesiarch's words.

"I am a monster?"

"No my friend. It is not your fault. I cannot imagine the things you have endured. It would be enough to unravel even the most stable mind. You are a creature of two very different parts and I am ashamed to say I have used your violent self to help in my missions.

"Are we friends?" asked Ortig.

"Yes of course we are."

"Then that's what friends do. They help each other. I cannot remember ever having another friend, so I will stay."

Srisk placed his hand on the giant's shoulder.

"I promise I will not de-activate the collar unless you wish me to do so."

"Thank you" said Ortig.

*

Mai'Len was one of the more well known planets that was lost to Dark Space during the Moretti war. It had been the celebrated location of the Federation's latest experiment in planetary seeding. It had been one of several candidates that were identified with the required celestial surroundings such as an orbiting moon, protective larger planets and a stable star, that would help sustain life.

They had taken a barren world devoid of all life and installed massive atmospheric generators, gravitational beacons, core plumes and introduced a primitive bio-sphere. The hope was to create an environment that could support sentient life. The Federation had achieved smaller successes with other planets, but most already had atmospherics or some form of bio-diversity. Mai'Len was the first to be created from nothing, the first world where the Federation had effectively played God. It was ironic that their shining example had never been populated as the blue and green planet lay outside the Defensive Necklace. It had been left to evolve under its own devices for the last few thousand years. So it had seemed a fitting location for the Keteran forces to start their offensive against the Moretti. History of the lost planet would tell a different story.

The small tug warped into high orbit behind the gas giant Via'Mhal. Srisk had expected to wait in the huge planet's shadow and intercept the armada as it made its way from the eighth gate. He had gambled that a simple demonstration of the dummy blink drives they had onboard would be enough to make them turn back or at least prepare for what lay ahead. They were too late.

The long range scanners on the Desolation lit up with white noise. The deep space antenna was receiving thousands of contacts. Some winked in and out of existence whilst other targets continued to flood on the periphery of the display. The tug ignited all four thrusters. Liktus set a trajectory that skimmed close to the massive gaseous planet and gave the sluggish craft a slingshot effect. As they rounded towards Mai'Len the star beyond silhouetted the unfolding scene.

The Keteran armada was vast. There were four super-massive battle-cruisers, each one carrying enough firepower to pulverise a small planet. Accompanying these leviathans of the stars was a mixture of destroyers, stellar-frigates and dreadnoughts. There were dense squadrons of star-clippers and well armed gunsweepers. Added to this was a myriad of ancillary craft and swarms of small fighter units. The armada was at least five thousand strong. The entire naval power of a Prime world on any other day would have been a magnificent sight to behold.

The full extent of the waiting Moretti force had not yet been fully realised. Their dark-hulled craft seemed as though they completely filled the void between Mai'Len and the inner system moon of Po'Ten. Thousands were already engaging the Keterans, but at least ten thousand more were lurking patiently, like predators waiting for their prey to weaken.

The Keteran navy had quickly learned of the Noxvata's deception. Several of the quicker stellar-frigates had turned to run, hoping to engage the blink drives and emerge behind the Defensive Necklace in safety. Instead they found they remained clearly in the pursuing Moretti's crosshairs and in their haste to make an escape the shield-less craft were being torn apart.

The Moretti fleet swarmed like insects around a dying animal. As soon as a Keteran vessel lost power or had its shields compromised, they pounced. The Moretti craft were a stark contrast to the smooth symmetrical lines of the Prime world's navy. Jagged spikes, haphazard protrusions, segmented fuselages and chaotic weapon systems formed black skinned ships that looked as if they had evolved rather than been designed. Green and violet light speckled their hulls giving them the appearance of a ghastly viral plague.

The Moretti command vessels were amorphous lumps; formed by smaller craft melded together like a twisted volcanic outpouring. No two ships were the same. Even the wasp-like fighters had infinite variations of weapons, wings and power plants.

From his relatively safe distance it was difficult for Srisk to gauge who had the upper hand. To the Keteran's credit they had rallied well after the initial shock. The smaller destroyers and frigates were keeping close to the monstrous battle-cruisers affording them some protection from the flagship's potent arsenal. The more manoeuvrable dreadnoughts attacked the enemy head on. Lances of white light pulsed into the Moretti horde. They were so many it was impossible to miss. The space between the larger ships was filled with combusting ordinance and fighter craft from both sides. They pivoted, rolled, stalled and jostled for position. One on one battles tested each pilot's mettle, but often became unbalanced as dozens more Moretti joined in or worse still they were annihilated in the overpowering crossfire.

The first sign of ascendancy came as the Desolation reached the debris strewn outfields of the battle.

The Keteran battle-cruiser, Star of Truth, had suffered catastrophic damage and a torus of ignited gas expanded outwards from its midsection. The massive ship bucked as its back was broken. The following explosion was like a condensed supernova. The blackness of space was temporarily replaced by a heavenly pulse of light. The resulting destructive force immolated the craft that had clung to her sides for protection. As the Star of Truth died it took hundreds more with it as its death throes cascaded through the closely packed fleet.

Srisk watched through the cramped cockpit in saddened awe. How could such a magnificent creation, with so many souls, die in such a futile and ugly manner. He opened a Recit channel to the crew.

"I think we will concede that our plan to turn back the armada may now be slightly optimistic. Although we still have that option."

"We're here now." Aleksy was sitting in the forward gun turret and sounded excited. "It's like we're the guest at the party that nobody invited, that nobody likes and that nobody cares if we leave. Then all of a sudden 'Kool and the Gang' come on the sound system, we start busting some serious moves, and it's like we're the heart and soul."

"Does anyone have any idea what he is talking about?" said Srisk.

[Probably another Terran reference] tapped Seelia.

"It's Earth not Terra. You'd think we'd be allowed to name our own planet!" exclaimed Aleksy.

[How do you know it is yours?] typed Seelia.

"Hang on" said Aleksy.

Suddenly the ship lurched as a Moretti fighter exploded in close proximity and the wreckage bounced off the tugs armour plating.

"Wahoo!" screamed Aleksy. "First Blood to me. I've always wanted to say that. Before you lot say anything, we are keeping count this time."

[Alek, I think you've eaten too much of that meat protein]

The graffiti daubed space-tug entered into the fray with its old but powerful guns blazing. The multi-layered caustic rounds were slowed by the Moretti's energy shields but it did not stop them. The explosive tips ripped vast gashes in the larger black ships and those that caught the swirling fighters, turned each one into a pyrotechnic display of gas and flame.

Aleksy's enhanced physiology gave him almost superhuman reactions and his linked retina targeting system allowed him to take out even the most stubborn and skilful fighter pilots. Srisk and Seelia operated the rear turrets. Srisk's years of combat experience allowed him a controlled calm. The automatic iridium blast shield slid down as a Moretti vessel imploded and the resulting pulse of light washed over the Desolation. Not that Srisk's eyes needed any protection from the blinding radiance. Seelia's gun pod swivelled quickly as she tracked a spluttering fighter in a high arc. She didn't have the technological advantages of the others, she relied on instinct.

Liktus came through on the Ecclesiarch's personal Recit channel.

" Master, I have established a link with the Obsidian Storm."

"Good. Patch me through."

"Who is this?" blurted the clearly impatient operator.

"If you want to see the end of this day, then put me through to the Admiral, or whoever is now in charge" demanded Srisk. A loud explosion sounded in the background followed by screaming and associated chaotic chords.

"I don't recognise your beacon signal. You are not part of the fleet. Identify yourself."

"My name is Ecclesiarch Srisk. Just tell the Admiral I was at the Battle of Epoch."

"Wait" came the curt reply.

As the Ecclesiarch patiently counted the seconds in the delay he saw the long boom of a Moretti Devourer appear in his periphery.

"Liktus. Get us away from that thing."

"Yes Master."

The Desolation's four engines swivelled and then a sudden burn sent them scurrying away from the monstrous black ship that started to swallow the Keteran fleet in its mechanical maw. The comms connection bleeped on Srisk's head-up display.

"This is Admiral Canu. My operator tells me you are a survivor of Epoch. If that is indeed true, then I have a moment for you soldier, but only a moment, as you can imagine my time is pressed." Despite the overwhelming despair of the situation the voice was articulate and level.

"Of course Admiral. I am a veteran of many encounters with the Moretti. I would offer some advice."

"Let's hear it, I'll gladly take anything at this point."

"This Moretti force is lead by a Guardian called Goshen' Foran. As you may know the Moretti will not fight without a leader. I would suggest your best chance is to find his location and then focus everything you have on it."

"That will be easier said than done, but thank you for your advice Ecclesiarch Srisk. Unfortunately I am getting reports from the Hex-bloks that have landed on Mai'Len that there is also a heavy Moretti presence planet-side. The Guardian may be there."

Srisk thought about the problem.

"If you can clear my ship and my crew with your ground forces, I'll take a look" offered Srisk.

"Ecclesiarch. Isn't that a title bestowed on those who are in the service of the Noxvata?" asked the Admiral.

"That it is. I am no longer of their employ."

"Very well. I do not have time to question your motives. I will clear access with the Overstrators inside the Hex-blocks. If you find any sign of the Guardian on the planet relay it to my command immediately so that we can commence an aerial bombardment. Don't be anywhere near it when it happens. Good luck soldier."

The Recit muted just as the small tug barrelled to the side. A flaming Keteran fighter had collided with the forward starboard engine. Alarms sounded throughout the antiquated ship. Aleksy had zoned out completely. He didn't hear the high pitch klaxon or see the crimson warning lights that illuminated the ladder-well beneath him. Aleksy squeezed the triggers and another Moretti fighter evaporated under the hailstorm of bullets.

From out of the debris came another. It had masked its approach in the wake of the first and now its plasma guns scorched the shield of the Desolation. Aleksy cursed under his breath as he tried to target the twisting trajectory of the fast approaching ship. The two craft exchanged fire but the more modern weapons of the Moretti blasted through the energy shield of the old tug and ripped into the armour plating. A few more seconds and the burning shots would have ruptured the hull but Aleksy's accuracy punched holes through the Moretti cockpit and the fighter became a swirling fireball. Worryingly the burning craft was tumbling directly towards the Desolation.

"Liktus, dive!" cried Aleksy.

The tug strained under the demands being placed on it and despite the engines' best efforts to push the craft into clear space the Moretti debris smashed into the fore-guard. Aleksy closed his eyes and instinctively brought his hands over his head as the dark metal wreckage scraped over the hull. It tore the antenna and starboard fin from their moorings before ripping a huge gash in the thick plating. As the fragmenting Moretti ship tumbled overhead a trailing beam clattered against Aleksy's gun blister.

He peered through his fingers as he heard the snick in the glass dome. He watched as the tiny spec quickly grew into a cobweb of white lines and the crackling sound intensified. Aleksy checked his harness straps and then reached for his emergency oxygen mask. He slapped himself on the forehead as he realised he had no need for it.

"Umm Liktus. I have a bit of a problem" said Aleksy nervously watching the spreading damage across the transparent dome.

"It will have to wait" replied Liktus. "Our shields are gone. Engine two has had it and four is failing fast. Another direct hit and it's game over. I am struggling to control the ship at all."

"Take us down to the planet" instructed Srisk.

"I will if I can Master" replied Liktus.

"The glass on my turret is about to shatter!" shouted Aleksy.

"Can you make it back into the ship?" asked Srisk.

"I'm not sure. It could go any second" panicked Aleksy.

"Liktus. Seal it off."

"What? How do I get out?"

"We can't risk breaching the ship's integrity. You'll have no problem breathing. Each gun pod has an ejector. When we reach the high atmosphere you'll automatically be thrown clear. We'll meet you on the surface of Mai'Len" instructed Srisk.

"Brilliant" moaned Aleksy as sarcastically as he could muster.

G-force churned the human's organs as the Desolation powered towards the planet. Liktus pulled on the controls desperately trying to avoid the metallic storm of debris raining down beside them from the battle in the stars. The glass dome covering Aleksy's gun pod couldn't withstand the pressure of the descent and finally shattered into a million crystal pieces. Aleksy gasped as the air around him was sucked into the vacuum. He watched as the tiny pieces of hardened glass trailed off towards the light show above. It reminded him of a fireworks display only less artistic and a lot colder.

He turned his head as another of the Keteran battle-cruisers spilled its innards into the void and its density drives flared briefly before it exploded like the birth of another new star.

This was all getting very real for the human passenger. Millions of lives were being lost as every new explosion lit up the sky. It had been the most exciting adventure to start with, but the close call with the Moretti fighter had shocked him. He had stared the reality of death in the face and the hopelessness of the situation was beginning to dawn on him. It was the first time since he had left his home that he truly believed that he would never see the Earth again. Aleksy searched his soul for courage and thankfully his sense of humour returned to comfort him.

"Anything I shoot down now counts as two" he voiced over the Recit.

Seelia replied. Her text scrolled across his forearm display.

[How many have you got so far?]

"The last one that exploded over me made eleven" said Aleksy with renewed confidence.

[Fourteen for me] typed Seelia.

"How can you have got that many? It doesn't matter how big they are you know they still all count as one. What about you Srisk? How many did you get?"

"I did not keep count. It would be childish to do so" replied the Ecclesiarch.

[He had six] recorded Seelia.

"It was seven actually" added Srisk.

Aleksy chuckled but his laughter trailed off into a long scream as the gun pod fasteners exploded and the gun unit was ejected from the smoking tug.

*

As the large chutes opened overhead Aleksy relaxed a little. The slower descent was a welcome relief from the pandemonium that had preceded. He looked around to see burning and smoking debris falling all around him. Interspersed within the mechanical confetti were the Hex-bloks from the battle-cruisers. Some were damaged. Scorch marks scoured the metal walls and one or two tumbled uncontrollably as their landing jets had been damaged. Together the Moretti and Keteran jetsam drifted through the atmosphere of Mai'Len towards the vast blue expanse below.

It wasn't until Aleksy was only a few thousand metres from splash down that he realised the extensive blue ocean was not actually water at all. It was grass. Tall thin blue blades that shimmered in the wind giving the impression of eddies and currents. The grass sea extended over the horizon in all directions except one. The bright azure savannah merged into a lush green island. As Aleksy drifted closer he could see huge trees that covered an island of jagged rock that lay beneath them. If it weren't for the pockets of burning wreckage that festered like sores within the immense blue field it would have been a wondrous sight.

*

The Hex-bloks were a masterpiece of Keteran engineering. The multipurpose craft had been duplicated by almost every other Prime world of the Federation. They were composed of a six sided faceted cylinder that doubled as a lifeboat as they jettisoned from the battle-cruisers and once landed they formed an impressive defensive outpost.

Powerful orange flame poured from the six engines located on each corner of the bloks. They stabilised the landing, bringing it neatly down into the blue grass. As the massive caterpillar tracks on its underside touched the soil, the jets switched off and they began to fold into the thirty foot walls of the Hex-blok. Secondary engines rumbled into life and the awkward vehicle began to trundle across the field flattening the grass.

Two of the units met. They were piloted so that two of the tall walls met in a parallel fashion. Cables fired from both bloks and hydraulic arms pulled the two pieces together. Metal mortise and tenon joints locked into place as more of the hexagon shaped bloks joined to form a honeycombed defensive line. Gun turrets rose into view above the high walls as the ingenious structure came online.

All across the grass ocean clusters of Hex-Bloks formed together. Those that had been damaged in the battle above or during the fall from space churned gears in a desperate attempt to rejoin the growing hubs. They were like expelled cells following their inbuilt instinct to return to the nucleus. Apparently there was safety in numbers.

*

Aleksy's ejector unit glided peacefully into the long grass. He was out and running before the canopy folded over the broken blister turret. He had seen the Desolation land close to the tree-line and next to a forming unit of Hex-bloks. He swiped the nav display on his comms unit and as Srisk had showed him he fixed directional coordinates.

The long blades of grass towered overhead. They were about eight feet tall. Aleksy was blinded by the blue vegetation. As he pushed his way through the wavering field he cycled through his internal systems. He stopped as he discovered a scan option. He discounted the visual settings and moved instead to the audio options. There was a list of unknown filters - words for which he had no understanding. He assumed they had some scientific meaning. A linear scale was labelled sensitivity. He mentally pushed the slider to the 'high' limit. Suddenly he spun around as he heard a footstep crunch the vegetation. He reached for his combat knife. His hearing had become acute. He could hear his own heart beat. The sound quickened in his chest.

He heard it again. It was the unmistakeable thud of footsteps. They were heading towards him. He couldn't see anything. He crouched low and waited, straining to see through the forest of blue blades. Then the dark shadow appeared.

Aleksy knew instantly it was a Moretti soldier. Srisk's description of them had been enough for the human to recognise the white bone carapace that crept towards him. Holding the serrated knife firmly in his hand Aleksy rushed forward. A deafening shot sailed by his head and he mentally adjusted his hearing once again before leaping into the air. He surprised the Marauder who managed to raise his arm against Aleksy's attack. The wide blade of the knife stabbed through the bone shell of the Marauder's forearm and exited the other side. The power in Aleksy's strike forced the Moretti's arm back and the tip of the blade punctured his chest plate. The bone clad soldier grunted as the metal blade stabbed into its flesh. A clawed hand thrust out and grabbed Aleksy around the throat. The powerful Moretti warrior lifted the human effortlessly from the floor. Aleksy stared into its black soul-less eyes. The Marauder squeezed its fingers trying to snap Aleksy's neck. It looked confused as the dangling human remained alive. Aleksy's bio-shield had activated. He reached out and pulled his knife free. Greenish-brown blood spurted into his face as the blade tore free. Aleksy rammed the knife upwards. It skewered the outstretched wrist of the soldier. The fingers opened and Aleksy dropped to the floor.

Aleksy shuffled forward and punched the inside of the Moretti's left knee and then the right. The power of the blows stunned the Marauder. It buckled and fell forward. Aleksy had shattered both knee joints. The human jumped backwards as the Marauder fell face first into the flattened grass. Aleksy grabbed the creature's rifle and ripped it from its blood soaked hand. He rammed the muzzle into the back of the Moretti's head and pulled the trigger. He cursed as it clicked harmlessly. Aleksy remembered Srisk's words. 'Only a Moretti can fire a Moretti weapon'.

Aleksy was about to retrieve his knife when a high velocity shot hit him high in the shoulder. The high powered round took him from his feet and threw him almost six metres back into the long grass. Warnings echoed in his head and he tried to move. He looked up to see the white bone mask of another Marauder loom over him. A heavy foot thumped onto his chest pinning him to the ground. The black eyes seemed to scan him with suspicion.

"Orgen vat sey" hissed the creature.

"Bite me" said Aleksy between clenched teeth.

The creature cocked its head to one side as if contemplating the fate of its prey. Without warning the Marauder's head flipped back. A fountain of fetid blood gushed from the sizeable hole in its forehead. Aleksy scrambled to his feet as the silver skinned figure of Seelia came running through the grass towards him. She lowered the barrel of her still smouldering sniper rifle.

"Are you okay?" she asked.

"I am now" smiled Aleksy.

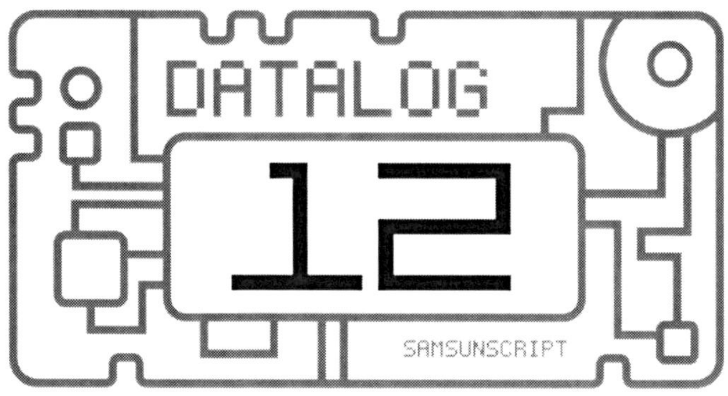

Planet-fall

Srisk looked out of the central control tower. The admiral had been true to his word and the acting commander of this particular Hex-blok had welcomed the Ecclesiarch, Ortig and Liktus inside. The junior officer was only too glad to share the burden of command as the assigned Overstrator had been killed in the hazardous descent.

Srisk was admiring the construction of the joined units. Soldiers were busy shifting ordinance, manning the walls and preparing the Quadraceptors for battle. Snipers were positioned on the outer walls and the plethora of gun turrets cycled through start up routines. The Keteran forces were able to move between the linked hexagons in similar shaped openings at the base of each wall or by the walkways that touched at the top.

"I've heard much about these constructs, Captain. I have to say I'm impressed."

Srisk turned to the immaculately turned out soldier. He could see the apprehension in his equally crisp facial expression. He was too young to have ever seen action. He was fresh from the Keteran academy of war. To his credit he had done a thorough job of mobilising the forces at his disposal. The Hex-blok stood ready to repel the inevitable.

"How many bloks do we have?" asked Srisk.

"Only thirteen in this compound Sir. Many were damaged when the Star of Truth was lost."

"What is your name Captain?" Srisk could see the young officer was struggling to keep a control on his emotions.

"Olsen Sir. Mayflower Olsen."

Srisk couldn't help but pause.

"My parent's idea of humour Sir. Not funny I know." admitted the Captain.

"It will have given you character if nothing else" said Srisk. "I'm not going to lie to you Captain Olsen. This is going to get ugly. The Moretti will be upon us as soon as they learn of our location. I can promise you we will give as good as we get. You must promise me to keep a level head. Can you do that?"

"Yes Sir" The captain saluted with renewed confidence and duty.

"Do you have details of the rest of the Keteran ground forces?" asked Srisk.

"We are reporting twenty-eight compounds but I do not have the figures for the associated composition of Hex-bloks. I can find out for you?" suggested the Captain.

"That won't be necessary. Can you connect me to the Overstrator in charge of this combined compound?"

The young Captain hesitated.

"What's the problem Captain Olsen?" asked Srisk.

"They are still in discussion Sir. Those that survived. There is some confusion on who has seniority."

"Put me on a visual link" demanded Srisk. "In the meantime, coordinate with the other bloks and raise the shields. If the battle for the stars is lost then we can expect an aerial assault."

The central screen flickered and the cabal of Overstrators appeared. A tall grey-haired individual looked into the camera.

"What is it? We are busy..." His voice trailed off as the hooded visage of Srisk filled his monitor feed. "Who might you be?" asked the man.

"I am an advisor" said Srisk carefully. "Admiral Canu personally asked me to oversee preparations planet-side. I am disappointed to see that you are all hiding inside when you should be standing in front of your men and organising the defence of this compound."

"There are protocols to follow. We must establish the hierarchy of command" complained the grey-haired Overstrator.

"You are at war!" blared Srisk. "There will be time to talk if you ever make it off this damned world. Let me make this simple. I am in command. I want each of you to return to your units and report any weaknesses in our defences immediately. The Moretti will not wait gentlemen. They will rip your beating hearts from your chests without thinking. Now set to your duties."

Srisk cut the feed before they could reply. He looked at the shocked Captain.

"I learnt my debating skills from the best" said Srisk quietly. The Ecclesiarch looked out of the window at the four-legged Quadraceptor that was being loaded with ammunition. "Captain. Why aren't those heavy units already out in the field?"

"They require specialised pilots Sir. Many were required to man the fighter squadrons when we first encountered the Moretti horde in orbit. We have lost so many good soldiers" he sighed. "I want to deploy them, but we have very few with the required skill set. Of those working we only have three piloted and ready to walk."

"Get them into the field as soon as you can Captain. I will take the one below. There is another in my team that has the required proficiency. When he arrives sort him out a ride."

Srisk turned to leave the command unit but stopped as he reached the door.

"Get those shields up Captain, and Captain."

"Yes sir."

"Say a prayer to whatever entity you believe in that we will see victory this day."

"We will win won't we sir?"

"Of course we will" lied Srisk.

The Ecclesiarch strode out into the compound where Liktus and Ortig were waiting. Liktus was clearly excited. He hopped from one foot to the other.

"Please tell me we are going to get to drive one of those Master."

The small red creature pointed up at the mighty Quadraceptor.

"We are. Go and get acquainted with the controls my friend. We leave forthwith."

"I already know how to drive one" replied Liktus.

"Of course you do" conceded the Ecclesiarch.

"What about me?" asked Ortig. "What do you want me to do?"

The stone-skinned giant rocked his head from side to side so that his cheeks touched the collar around his neck.

"You want to switch it off. Don't you?"

"No my friend" replied Srisk. "That is not necessary. When the fighting starts there will be heavy casualties. It is essential that these units hold. The wall guns will need resupply. I would ask that you stay here and help where you can."

Ortig formed an awkward smile.

"I help here."

The goliath turned and lifted an ammunition crate from the floor. A soldier in a mechanised lifter stared at the stone giant.

"Where does it go?" asked Ortig.

"Follow me" said the Keteran soldier.

Srisk turned his forearm over and tapped into his console.

[Have you found him?]

[Yes. On our way back now] came the reply.

[Is he in one piece?]

[Of sorts] replied Seelia.

[Liktus and I are headed out to meet the enemy. Join us when you get here. I think Alek might like this new toy.]

*

The Keteran military had developed a huge arsenal of equipment and vehicles but the Quadraceptor remained the undisputed favourite. It was affectionately known as the 'King Walker'.

It consisted of a central body unit that was supported high above the ground by four enormous hydraulic legs. Mounted on its armoured back carapace were a series of rocket tubes that gave it a spiky silhouette. A large calibre plasma carbine hung under the nose and under the belly hung the main gun. The massive Volt cannon packed the same firepower that would usually be found attached to most star craft. The spider-like vehicle was agile and could easily traverse most environments. It was a proven weapon of war and Liktus beamed as he moved it forwards. The door in the Hex-blok wall folded in on itself allowing the walker to step over it and thud into the blue field beyond.

The Keteran forces had tried to provide a killing ground around the compound by attempting to burn the blue grass. They had discovered that the strange vegetation was naturally fire resistant. The tall leaves withered under the intense heat but the fire did not spread. Despite their best effort the grass remained at full height only twenty metres away from the honeycomb base. When the Moretti attacked, there would be very little notice.

As the gates closed behind the armoured walker, the first shots of the battle for Mai'Len echoed across the grass ocean.

The Moretti swarmed through the azure meadow firing as they ran. The turret guns of the compound barked their reply and the auto-cannons obliterated the charging line. The air was filled with chunks of flesh as the defenders maintained a constant bullet storm.

Srisk sat in the chin gun of the Quadraceptor. He could see the white and black shapes running randomly through the cover of the grass. He squeezed the trigger and ploughed a channel of destruction. The Moretti ran from the outpouring but Srisk rotated the weapon chasing them down. He glanced down to see figures milling around one of the legs.

"They are beneath us. They will try and disable a leg and take us down."

"I'm on it Master" replied Liktus.

Swirls of electricity flickered from a node on each leg and then in an instant a high voltage grid sprang into life between them. It fried the Moretti soldiers caught in its grasp and effectively cut the grass in a neat square.

A sound like distant thunder rolled across the grasslands. A high powered shell landed just short of the compound and a column of soil, blue leaves and Moretti bodies erupted into the air. The loss of their own soldiers under friendly fire was an accepted fact of war.

"Where did that come from?" asked Srisk.

Liktus was already side stepping the giant mechanical walker when another missile sailed overhead. This time it hit the compound. To Srisk's relief, multicoloured circles rippled across the shield surface like oil on water.

"Three twenty degrees" said Liktus.

Srisk magnified his scope view.

"Onager" cursed Srisk.

"What are they?" asked Liktus.

"Bad news" replied Srisk. "Get a fix on it. We have to take it out."

The metal legs stamped up and down as the Quadraceptor tried to get into a firing position. The massive Volt cannon pulsed and the machine's back legs were pushed into the ground from the force of the shot.

"Did we hit it?" asked Srisk

"No Master. It's moving incredibly fast."

"We need to get closer."

"Yes Master. Just a moment."

The electric net between the legs materialised again burning another square and passing six thousand volts through the Moretti soldiers that were caught within its borders. The two front legs of the Quadraceptor then reared up and the armoured killing machine leapt forward in an insect like charge. As they closed the distance the horror of the Onager came into view.

The Moretti had their own armoured corps and they utilised vehicles where they gave an advantage but their genius lay in the use of beasts. Onagers were colossal six-legged titans. Their bodies were covered in chitin armour similar to their Moretti masters. The heavy set head ended in a vicious curved horn. Strapped high on its back the Moretti had mounted a concussion mortar and packed inside the platform around it were dozens of well armed Thornbred warriors. They hooted and wailed as the bullish monster charged across the undulating blue sea of grass, towards the mechanical insect that scurried to meet it.

Srisk kept the nose gun trained on the creature and blasted a series of holes in its natural armour. The Moretti strapped to its back were shielded and it shimmered as it absorbed the gunfire. The Onager was running in a arc towards the Quadraceptor. Either it or the Moretti Resonator in control was trying to avoid running head on towards its enemy. It realised the power of the belly-slung weapon waiting to bring it down.

The Volt cannon thundered as Liktus tried to manoeuvre into position. The shot only succeeded in blasting a few fins and bony horns from the Onager's back. It didn't even notice the wound.

"It's too quick" called Srisk. "It's trying to get behind us."

"I know Master" said Liktus. "I have a plan."

The Ecclesiarch shook his head as he tried to keep his gun trained on the rampaging creature. The legs of the Quadraceptor thumped up and down as it sought to turn. The speed of the Onager took it safely away from the main weapon and it rounded behind the stamping machine. It lowered its head preparing to charge with its long curved horn. Just as it neared, Liktus put his plan into operation. He thumped the machine's controls and then held onto his seat as the four legs all withdrew in unison. The massive mechanoid leapt vertically into the air. The Onager charged harmlessly beneath it. As the forty tonne machine came back to the ground Liktus raised the front limbs and then plunged them down. The Quadraceptor's armoured metal legs sank into the back of the beast pinning it to the spot. The Volt cannon boomed and the Onager was vaporised from point blank range.

"Well done Liktus" applauded Srisk.

As the large steaming slabs of flesh slid across the cockpit glass Liktus operated the windshield scrubbers. As they removed the Onager blood and detritus he got his first glimpse of the Moretti force.

"Umm Master."

"I see them" replied the Ecclesiarch.

The earth shook as at least twenty more of the colossal beasts rampaged towards them.

*

Aleksy stared at the complex controls. There were two multi-function joysticks both of which had mini control sticks for each finger-tip, there was an array of voice prompts and finally there were retina commands that could be used on the display that was overlaid onto the cockpit glass. Aleksy understood why this vehicle required exacting dexterity and a unique set of skills. He looked into his mind and accepted the request to connect to the Quadraceptor. As his fingers touched the controls the machine lurched forwards on its forelegs.

[Are you sure you can drive this thing?]

"You're welcome to swap places" suggested Aleksy. He toggled one of the mini-joysticks and the front of the vehicle levelled out. It took a few more unstable steps before miraculously the novice human pilot had the complex walker thudding out into the field.

The fighting had seen a lull from the initial attack. The young Captain had suspected that it was simply the Moretti testing their defences before they launched their main campaign. Whatever the reason it gave Aleksy and Seelia the opportunity to enter the field without the expected stress of instant battle and gave them a chance to get a feel for the colossal machine.

A text string scrolled across the windscreen alerting Aleksy to an incoming communication.

"Yes Captain" answered Aleksy.

"How are you finding it?"

"I think I have the hang of it. It was a bit like Bambi on ice to start with but I'm in control now."

There was a moment's silence. Aleksy realised that the Captain would have no idea who or what Bambi was.

"Any response from Srisk?" asked Aleksy trying to move the conversation on.

"No nothing. His 'Quad' is still operational but we can't raise him on the Recit. Maybe they're having technical difficulties. Scans are picking up a lot of movement around him though. Maybe the Moretti are mobilising?"

"Maybe" said Aleksy. "Can you send me his last co-ordinates?"

"I can, but we are picking up three closer anomalies on our scans coming along the tree-line to the East. Could you recon that area before you head out after the Ecclesiarch?"

"Okay, we'll take a quick look. Alek out."

The four-legged machine thumped along next to where the tall blue grass thinned and the edge of the forest began. The wide canopies formed a dense umbrella of foliage that soared in the breeze way above the Quadraceptor. Aleksy kept looking towards the pencil-straight tree trunks expecting to see something move. He struggled to see any signs of life. The occasional bird would fly out from the blue meadow as the giant machine sounded its approach.

Three solid signals lit up on the long range proximity scan. Aleksy selected the zoom control and magnified the view from the left window. The screen filled with the image of a horned beast. As Aleksy moved the Quadraceptor to the left he saw two more identical animals. The bone and black Moretti soldiers were easily identifiable on their backs. They pumped their rifles in the air whilst clinging to the strapped platform with the other arm. They were clearly enjoying the rush of the ride.

Aleksy's finger hovered over the trigger of the main cannon. His enhanced brain instantly calculated the velocity, wind speed and trajectory. With a slight twitch of a finger joystick the walker jerked backwards as the deadly Volt cannon fired. Aleksy couldn't take his eyes off the screen. He grinned with a macabre satisfaction as the energy bolt thumped into the lead beast. The super-heated shot obliterated the animal's midsection and with it the riding Moretti Thornbred passengers. The forward motion of the creature caused it to buckle and Aleksy could see the remnants of the huge curved ribcage snap under the force.

The remaining two Onagers started to weave in an erratic path through the blue sea of grass. The mortars on their backs barked a reply and the alarms on Aleksy's head-up display started to track the incoming shells. The mechanical walker side stepped as the arcing ordinance fell a short distance away. Fountains of soil shot into the air as the mortar rounds formed a series of identical craters. The nose gun of the Quadraceptor opened up as Seelia noticed dozens of black and white figures rushing through the long grass.

Aleksy had to constantly recalculate his targeting vectors as the charging Onagers remained unpredictable in their approach. Several shots had already missed. The last blast had severed the end of the creature's tail but it didn't seemed to notice. They were rapidly closing the distance. The human pilot blocked out the constant chug of Seelia's chin gun and the returning small arms fire from the Moretti scurrying around the metal legs of the machine. Once again the Quadraceptor slid backwards as the Volt cannon boomed. The shot thundered across the plains but was a long way in front of the remaining beasts. The white hot bolt exploded in the forest line. The shot pulverised the trunk of a tall tree. As splintered flame shot out into the dense undergrowth a loud crack sounded. The tree toppled.

The charging Onagers desperately tried to avoid the falling object. The delicate leaves of the top canopy brushed the flanks of one animal but the other was flattened under the mountainous weight of the trunk. A tornado of leaves and dust formed a curtain of debris and horrific screams of the injured animal howled within.

Aleksy fired the cannon blind. The shot vanished into the dust cloud just as the long black horn of the remaining Onager charged out. Aleksy pulled on the controls trying to spin the machine but the animal was being expertly steered and only the bouncing tail appeared in the human's targeting reticule.

"I can't get a fix" shouted Aleksy. "Can you take out the Moretti on its back?"

Seelia aimed at the whooping soldiers but her shots skipped over the shield like pebbles skimming across a pond. The Onager quickly closed and with its head down rammed the four-legged walker. The force was immense. The front right leg hydraulics ruptured and the foot spike bent back on itself. As the Quadraceptor buckled forwards the creature used its massive neck muscles to drive the horn into the main body. Power drained as the beast punctured the core. Aleksy pulled the trigger one last time and the searing white bolt blew two of the Onager's back legs away. The close quarters shot sent the mechanical walker skidding backwards. It then nose dived into the long grass as all of the systems failed.

Aleksy reached out to Seelia with his mind.

< Let's get out of here, they'll be crawling over us in seconds >

< Already ahead of you. Oh and Alek >

< What? >

< Don't forget to bring your gun this time >

Aleksy cursed under his breath and reached back for the compact machine pistol strapped to the back of the pilot's seat. He turned the release handle on the emergency escape hatch and the door fell outwards. The square piece of metal thumped onto the bone-plated skull of a Marauder who had already arrived on the scene. Aleksy jumped. He landed on the discarded hatch just as the Moretti warrior was trying to rise.

< Where are you? >

< Running towards the tree-line. It's our best shot at getting back to the Hex-bloks > replied Seelia.

< On my way >

Aleksy ran into the tall grass just as shots pinged off the downed walker. The thwip thwip of bullets sounded in his ears as some of the tall fronds were cut down around him. Aleksy didn't look back. He knew they were right behind him. He used one hand to part the grass as he ran, the other was tightly clutched around his gun. Aleksy span quickly sending a wild volley of shots into the blueness. The fully automatic machine-pistol quickly emptied the chamber. Finally he reached the edge of the vast field. The grass stepped down in height and finally disappeared altogether as the huge root complex of the forest sucked all the nutrients from the ground. With his full periphery vision returned he then realised how close behind him the Moretti had been. Three leapt into the clearing.

Aleksy made to turn but his foot got caught in the folded grass stems and he tripped. He heard three shots and then Seelia call out to him.

"Stop messing about. Get a move on."

As Aleksy pushed himself up he glanced back to see all three Moretti warriors motionless. A single bullet hole in each skull.

"My God she's good" he said under his breath.

As Aleksy reached the forest a hailstorm of bullets started to shred the bark around him. He continued to run. His increased speed allowed him to catch up with the silver skinned woman. The blood-thirsty cries of the Moretti pushed them deeper into the woodland.

A short distance ahead they could see water vapour. It formed a long thin cloud within the forest. As they neared they could see the edge of a large chasm. The crack in the earth spread out in either direction as far as they could see. It was like a tectonic break. Aleksy placed his foot close the lip of the gorge and peered over. It was at least a hundred metres deep. A small stream meandered through the rocky bottom.

"Crap." Said Aleksy.

Seelia knelt down. She calmly pulled the sniper rifle trigger repeatedly. Each high-powered slug pitching a charging soldier from their feet. Her ammunition chamber clicked empty.

"Crap" she repeated.

Aleksy smiled. Seelia stood and threw her gun to the floor. She drew her combat knife. Aleksy copied her actions. The Moretti slowed as they realised their prey had nowhere to run. They would savour this kill. Guns and rifles were holstered and wide blades and crude axes glinted in the daylight. The front soldier was taller than the rest of the Marauders. He dipped his forefinger into a pouch on his belt. He wiped the red paste across his eyes, and then drew a symbol on the wide blade of his cleaver.

"Achor metaxis" he hissed and pointed towards the silver-skinned woman.

He suddenly ran. The big Moretti warrior collided with Seelia and they teetered on the edge. He tried to bring his pommel downward to disarm her, but the lithe woman twisted in his grip. The edge of the cleaver tore a hole in her combat-suit. Seelia ignored the pain and stabbed her knife into the Marauder's thigh. The Moretti soldier threw his head back in what could only be described as laughter. It reminded Aleksy of a hyena. He quickly brought his head forward smashing his forehead into Seelia's face. Blood pumped from the split across her nose. Seelia spat the crimson liquid into her attacker's face.

"If I'm going, then you're coming with me." She wrapped her legs around the Moretti's waist and leant backwards.

The situation had unfolded so quickly. Aleksy had blocked an initial strike and then jumped into the air kicking the soldier in the jaw knocking him out. He parried another vicious jab and then had lashed out with his knife tearing a gash in the Moretti's windpipe. He turned to see Seelia and the Marauder fall over the edge in their deathly embrace.

"No!" cried Aleksy.

He ran to the precipice and launched himself over the edge. Seelia had managed to untangle herself from the flailing Moretti warrior. She was falling on her back. She looked up and smiled as she saw Aleksy diving towards her.

"I'm sorry" she said quietly.

Tears streamed from Aleksy's eyes as the wind rushed past him and the ground came into focus below. He strained as he reached for Seelia's outstretched arms. Their hands met and Aleksy pulled Seelia close to his chest. He heard the thud as the Marauder's body broke on the stones beneath them. Aleksy closed his eyes. The air pulsed and buckled and with a static crackle the two inseparable bodies vanished into the mist.

*

The Volt cannon pushed Srisk's Quadraceptor further back with each shot. There were four deep furrows stretching from each of the walker's legs.

Srisk looked at his map display.

"Have you been able to raise the Captain?" he asked.

"No Master. Comms are off-line. They must have been damaged."

"We need to warn the bloks of what's coming their way."

At that moment a vee formation of black fighters roared overhead.

"We may be too late" said Liktus.

Srisk could hear them unleash their payloads on the shielded Hex-bloks.

"We won't make it back to the compound in time my friend, even with your driving ability. By the sound of it there may not be much to return to anyway. Unless this thing can fly we are going to make our stand here and now."

"I am ready Master" replied Liktus.

The lone walker kept firing until the wall of black beasts was on top of it. Four steaming Onager carcases lay dead. The electrified net that stretched between the legs had carved a large playing field as it had moved from side to side. Hundreds of Moretti bodies were interspersed with the freshly cut blue grass. More flooded from the edges of the area the walker had carved out. Srisk had to release the triggers as the nose gun overheated. It had been firing constantly for at least four minutes. One of the giant Onagers bounded into the clearing. It crushed several Thornbred soldiers in its eagerness to get to its target. Two more circled around behind the Quadraceptor.

Liktus edged the machine to the left. The six-legged beasts synchronised their attack. Liktus waited until the last moment and once again retracted the legs causing the machine to leap into the air. The Onager rushed beneath the Quadraceptor and its curved horn tore into the haunches of one of the others. As the walker landed one of its rear legs punched a hole in the back of the thrashing animal. The metal foot-spike drove deeply into its body and the creature roared in agony. It desperately tried to escape the pain and in doing so, its horn that was impaled in the shoulder of the second Onager, dug deeper and ripped sinew, bone and muscle before it erupted through the skin.

Having one leg stuck into the animal had caused the Quadraceptor to over-balance. Liktus fought the controls to try and stabilise the machine. At the same time he tried to free the trapped limb. Before he had a chance the remaining Onager collided with the walker. The force was incredible. Two of the legs buckled and snapped under the weight of the charge and the brave machine finally fell into the soil. The black beast reared up and its front legs pounded down repeatedly on the body of the Quadraceptor.

Liktus curled his arms and legs into his chair as the metal coffin closed around him. The final warning lights blinked out as the power core ruptured. Liktus pulled the lever to operate the mechanical fire suppressant. He hoped it would still work.

The small red creature climbed through the restricted space and squeezed through the deformed cockpit opening. Moretti soldiers were running towards the downed unit from all directions. The braying Onager had stopped as its passengers were also keen to parade their kill. Liktus slid across the wreckage and jumped down to where he could see Srisk's gauntleted arm sticking out from the crushed gunnery position. As he landed a Moretti Thornbred rounded the metal ruin. Liktus pressed his back into the hull and his skin instantly changed to mimic the colour of the Quadraceptor. The Moretti soldier did not see the camouflaged creature. The Thornbred ripped a panel away and then reached into the Ecclesiarch. He turned and shouted to his comrades.

"Essen at Molech. Mi con ultra-tarsus"

Liktus remained motionless with his eyes closed. He tried not to let the tear fall. He understood the Moretti's words.

"He is dead, We are too late."

*

The battle of stars above Mai'Len lasted another four days as the Keteran fleet held out to the very last. The final bastion of Hex-bloks fell eight days later. Mai'Len remained a Moretti world and once again Dark Space embraced the blue and green planet.

Epilogue

As the air fizzed, the surrounding wildlife scattered. Birds chirped and flew away from the forming rip in the atmosphere. The heat intensified and pressure soared before suddenly two bodies appeared and fell from the sky. They thudded into the lush green grass.

Aleksy rolled onto his back and groaned. He rubbed his head and sat up. Seelia lay next to him. Her eyes were wide open and she was staring up at the wispy clouds.

"You are insane" she said.

Aleksy helped her to her feet.

"Where are we?" she asked.

Aleksy looked around.

"I have a pretty good idea. I activated the blink drive. I think it has taken us back to the last location that was put into the system."

He held out his hand towards Seelia. She took it.

"Welcome to Earth" he said.

"It's more beautiful than I remember."

She looked at Aleksy. She could see the happiness etched across his face. She didn't want to ruin it. Seelia sighed deeply.

"You know I can't stay here don't you?" she said softly.

"Why not" said Aleksy instantly. "You'll love it here. There are no Moretti and not everyone will try and kill you, well not here in Wiltshire anyway."

Seelia smiled.

"Somehow I think I would be noticed."

"What do you mean?" pleaded Aleksy.

"Although I have grown to like your pale worm-like complexion I think my shining silver skin may make me stand out."

"That's a good point" conceded Aleksy. "I have got so used to you, I hardly notice."

"I need to leave." said Seelia.

"There has to be a way you can stay. I could say that you have some rare disease or that you are just a really keen cosplayer. Trust me there are plenty of people that look a lot stranger than you."

"I'm sure you mean that as a compliment, but you know that we can't stay. You are not the same person that left this place. You are no more human than I am." Seelia took Aleksy's other hand in hers. "When I said that I needed to leave, I meant, we."

Aleksy pulled her close to him. He looked into her eyes.

"Where shall we go?"

"You decide" replied Seelia.

Time and space folded in a sucking pop as the two warriors of the balance vanished, leaving the serene countryside scene as it had been only a moment before.

*

Liktus remained by the body of his Master. He had tried to pull him free from the mangled wreckage but he did not have the strength. He watched as squadrons of Moretti fighters tore across the sky blanket bombing the stubborn Keteran resistance.

On the third day of his vigil his heart had sunk. A long parade of Moretti soldiers trudged back from the smoking bloks. They had a line of Keteran prisoners tied together at the neck. Behind them in a makeshift cage sat the stone figure of Ortig. He looked afraid. The accompanying Thornbred soldiers poked their guns through the bars taunting the timid creature.

Liktus crawled through the stale blood of the Ecclesiarch and flipped open the cover to his forearm console. He tapped several of the buttons and then turned back to the line of despair. He watched in great satisfaction as Ortig smashed the cage into pieces. The stone behemoth ripped the head from one Marauder and used it to bludgeon another. Chaos ensued as Ortig tore away limbs and disembowelled others. As the first shots were fired the stone-skinned giant had already fled into the maze of tall grass.

Liktus smiled. He suddenly jumped as Srisk's finger moved.

"Master. Master" he called.

A faint orange glow illuminated the Ecclesiarch's hood.

"You are alive!" exclaimed Liktus

"Barely" croaked Srisk.

"I thought you were dead."

"I may have appeared that way. I shut down all non-essential systems. My body needed time to repair itself. What has happened to the others?"

"I don't know about Seelia or Alek but Ortig has finally found a home."

Srisk tried to laugh but only managed to splutter instead.

"What now Master?" asked Liktus.

The Ecclesiarch reached inside his cloak and took out the golden seal of the Noxvata. He wrapped the chain around his wrist.

"Now my friend, it is time for revenge."

<END>

About the Author

Samsun completed his first novel, Dying Star - Prophecy, in 2010 and hasn't stopped scribbling since. A professionally trained digital artist and instructional designer, he's worked in the games industry for 25 years and he pours this experience into his creative writing.

His early influences include David Gemmell , David Eddings and Michael Moorcock, and more recently some of the Warhammer 40k Black Library titles but what really drives him is his desire to create a unique story.

He's often asked how he comes up with the ideas for his books, and the truth is that he dreams them – often starting at the end and working his way back!

When he's not asleep (creative process) he runs a successful multimedia company in Somerset and lives with his wife, 2 children and a hyperactive puppy! He's an active supporter of the local football teams and pubs, he can also be found exploring new landscapes to base his worlds on whilst out and about on his quad bike.

Other titles by this author:

The Dying Star Trilogy

- Dying Star - Prophecy
- Dying Star - Exodus
- Dying Star - Darkness

The RUIN Saga

- Ruin - Birth of a Legend
- Ruin - Awakening
- Ruin - The Ghost Isle
- Ruin - The Nexus
- Ruin - The Creatures of the Orb (coming 2016)

Lightning Source UK Ltd.
Milton Keynes UK
UKOW01f1232280416

273152UK00002B/99/P